BONE

Out from Boneville

By Jeff Smith
with color by Steve Hamaker

graphix
An Imprint of
SCHOLASTIC

This book is for Vijaya

Library of Congress Cataloging-in-Publication Data is available.
ISBN-13: 978-0-439-70623-0 – ISBN-10: 0-439-70623-8 (hardcover)
ISBN 0-439-70640-8 (paperback)

ACKNOWLEDGMENTS

Harvestar Family Crest designed by Charles Vess
Map of *The Valley* by Mark Crilley

22 23 24 25 26 27 28 29 30 14 15 16
First Scholastic edition, February 2005
Book design by David Saylor
Printed in Singapore 46

CONTENTS

BONE
STILL NO SIGN OF THE TOWNSPEOPLE.
HEY! YA HEAR THAT, PHONEY? TH' COAST IS CLEAR!
LOOK AT HIM! WE GOT CHASED OUTTA BONEVILLE OVER TWO WEEKS AGO, AN' HE'S STILL MOPIN' AROUND!
...OH, WELL... I GUESS YOU CAN WHINE ALL YOU WANT, WHEN YER TH' RICHEST GUY IN TH' WHOLE TOWN.
AAAH!
OOPS! SILLY ME. EX-RICHEST!

DON'T GET HIM STARTED.
THEY CAN'T DO THIS TO ME! YOU CAN'T DO ANYTHING TO A RICH PERSON THAT HE DOESN'T WANT!
GASP! OH! TH' HORRIBLE INJUSTICE OF IT ALL! I'M STILL REELING WITH SHOCK!!
I'M A RESPECTED COMMUNITY LEADER! A SHINING PILLAR OF MORAL STRENGTH!
...SO A COUPLE OF SHADY BUSINESS DEALS WENT SOUR... IS THAT ANY REASON TO RUN TH' MOST BELOVED BONE IN BONEVILLE OUT ON A RAIL?!
YES.
BELOVED? TH' MAYOR DECLARED A SCHOOL HOLIDAY JUST SO TH' KIDS COULD COME AND THROW ROCKS AT YOU!
INGRATES!
OH, THEY'LL RUE TH' DAY THEY CHASED PHONCIBLE P. BONE OUTTA THEIR CRUMMY OL' TOWN!
SNIFF!
NOW, NOW, LITTLE BUCKAROO! DON'T BE SAD! IT'S A BEAUTIFUL DAY! THERE'S NOT A CLOUD IN TH' SKY!

THE MAP

GOOD POINT, SMILEY. IF WE DON'T FIND SOME SHADE SOON, I'M GONNA HAVE A STROKE!
HEY, I'M JUST TRYIN' TO CHEER HIM UP, OKAY?
TRY THINKIN' ABOUT SOMETHIN' BESIDES YOUR MONEY!
TAKE ME FOR EXAMPLE! I NEVER HAD A PENNY IN MY LIFE!
BUT I'M NOT SAD! I GOT NO RESPONSIBILITIES! I'M FREE! FREE AS A BIRD!
A BIRD? HA! MORE LIKE A MANGY, STRAY DOG WHO DOESN'T EAT VERY OFTEN!
WELL . . . TRUE! BUT YOU GET MY POINT!
HEY! FONE BONE!
WHAT?
HAVE YOU FIGURED OUT WHERE WE ARE, YET? WHAT'S TAKIN' SO LONG?
I'M WORKING ON IT. HMMMM . . . . THAT'S STRANGE... THAT MOUNTAIN RANGE ISN'T ON ANY OF OUR CHARTS - -

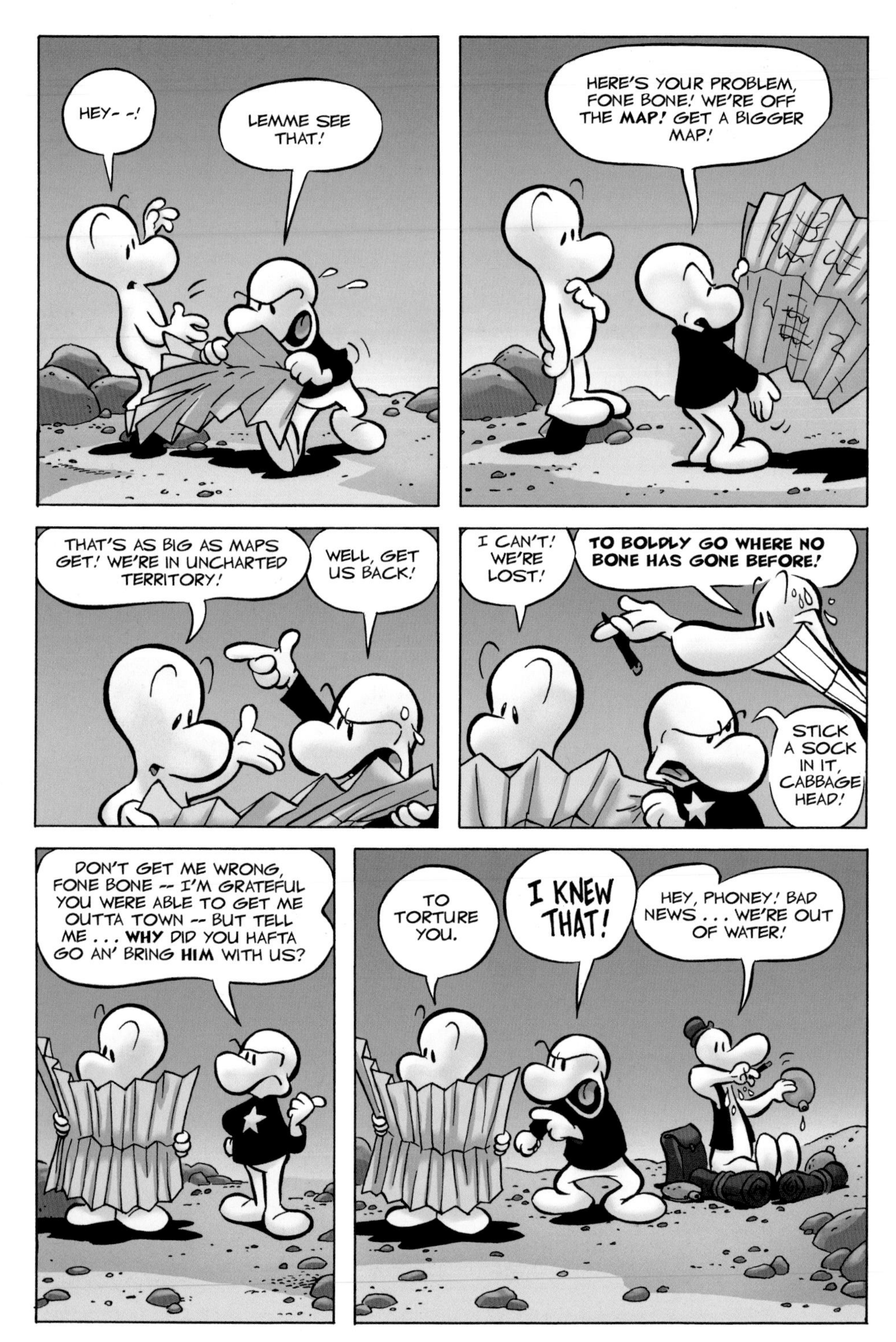
HEY- -!
LEMME SEE THAT!
HERE'S YOUR PROBLEM, FONE BONE! WE'RE OFF THE MAP! GET A BIGGER MAP!
THAT'S AS BIG AS MAPS GET! WE'RE IN UNCHARTED TERRITORY!
WELL, GET US BACK!
I CAN'T! WE'RE LOST!
TO BOLDLY GO WHERE NO BONE HAS GONE BEFORE!
STICK A SOCK IN IT, CABBAGE HEAD!
DON'T GET ME WRONG, FONE BONE -- I'M GRATEFUL YOU WERE ABLE TO GET ME OUTTA TOWN -- BUT TELL ME . . . WHY DID YOU HAFTA GO AN' BRING HIM WITH US?
TO TORTURE YOU.
I KNEW THAT!
HEY, PHONEY! BAD NEWS . . . WE'RE OUT OF WATER!

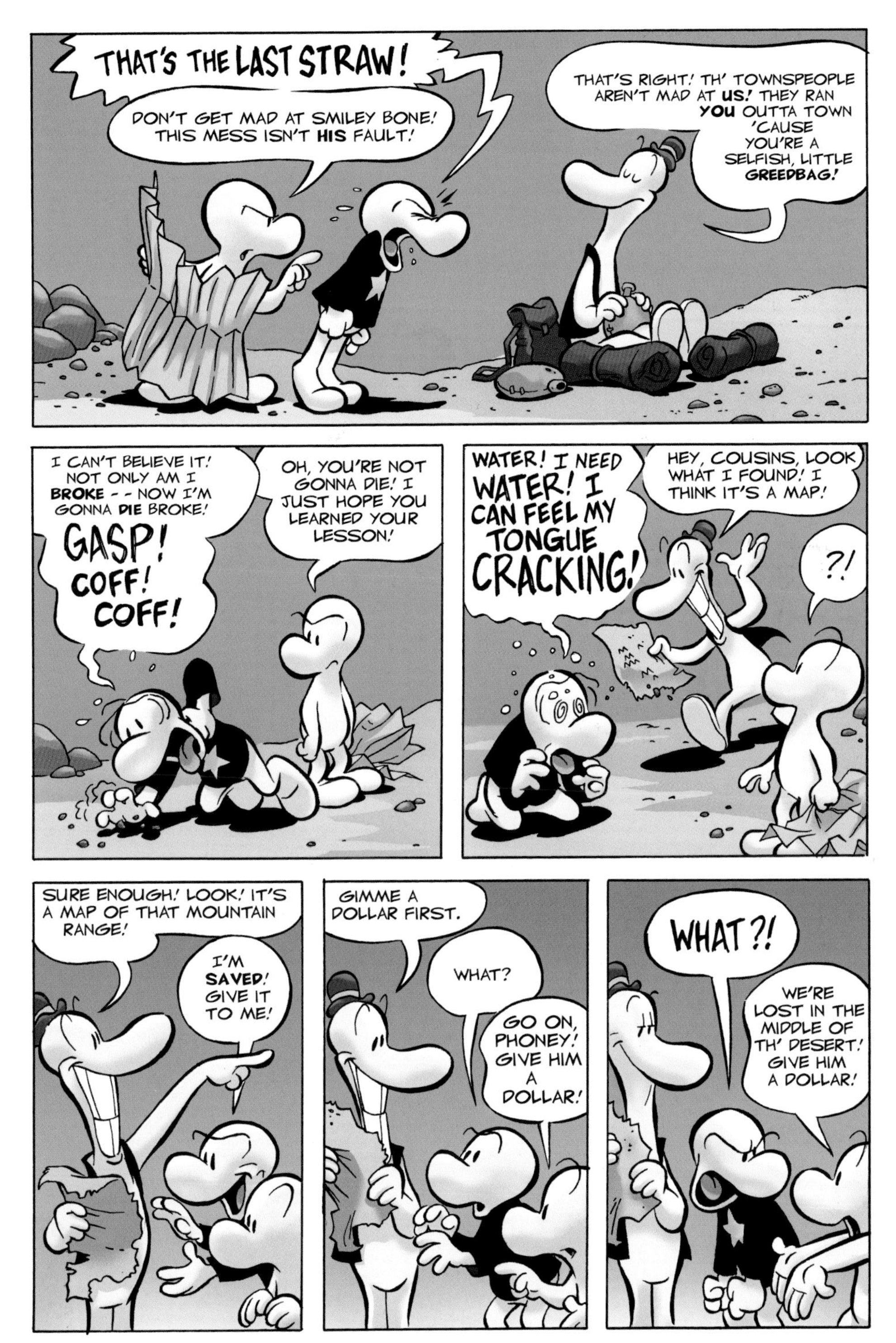

THAT'S THE LAST STRAW!
DON'T GET MAD AT SMILEY BONE! THIS MESS ISN'T HIS FAULT!
THAT'S RIGHT! TH' TOWNSPEOPLE AREN'T MAD AT US! THEY RAN YOU OUTTA TOWN 'CAUSE YOU'RE A SELFISH, LITTLE GREEDBAG!
I CAN'T BELIEVE IT! NOT ONLY AM I BROKE -- NOW I'M GONNA DIE BROKE! GASP! COFF! COFF!
OH, YOU'RE NOT GONNA DIE! I JUST HOPE YOU LEARNED YOUR LESSON!
WATER! I NEED WATER! I CAN FEEL MY TONGUE CRACKING!
HEY, COUSINS, LOOK WHAT I FOUND! I THINK IT'S A MAP!
?!
SURE ENOUGH! LOOK! IT'S A MAP OF THAT MOUNTAIN RANGE!
I'M SAVED! GIVE IT TO ME!
GIMME A DOLLAR FIRST.
WHAT?
GO ON, PHONEY! GIVE HIM A DOLLAR!
WHAT?!
WE'RE LOST IN THE MIDDLE OF TH' DESERT! GIVE HIM A DOLLAR!

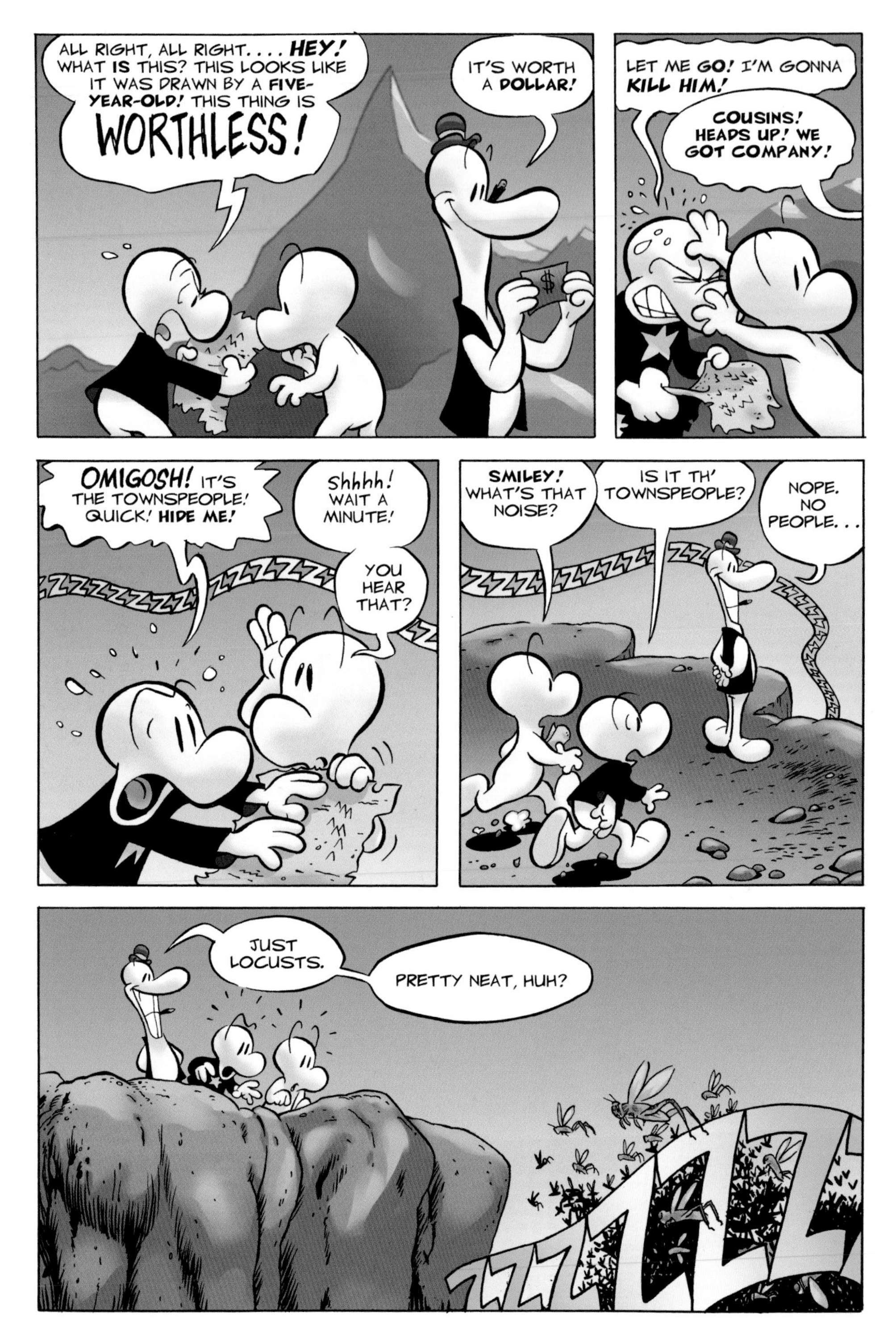
ALL RIGHT, ALL RIGHT. . . . HEY! WHAT IS THIS? THIS LOOKS LIKE IT WAS DRAWN BY A FIVE-YEAR-OLD! THIS THING IS WORTHLESS!
IT'S WORTH A DOLLAR!
LET ME GO! I'M GONNA KILL HIM!
COUSINS! HEADS UP! WE GOT COMPANY!
OMIGOSH! IT'S THE TOWNSPEOPLE! QUICK! HIDE ME!
Shhhh! WAIT A MINUTE!
YOU HEAR THAT?
SMILEY! WHAT'S THAT NOISE?
IS IT TH' TOWNSPEOPLE?
NOPE. NO PEOPLE. . .
JUST LOCUSTS.
PRETTY NEAT, HUH?

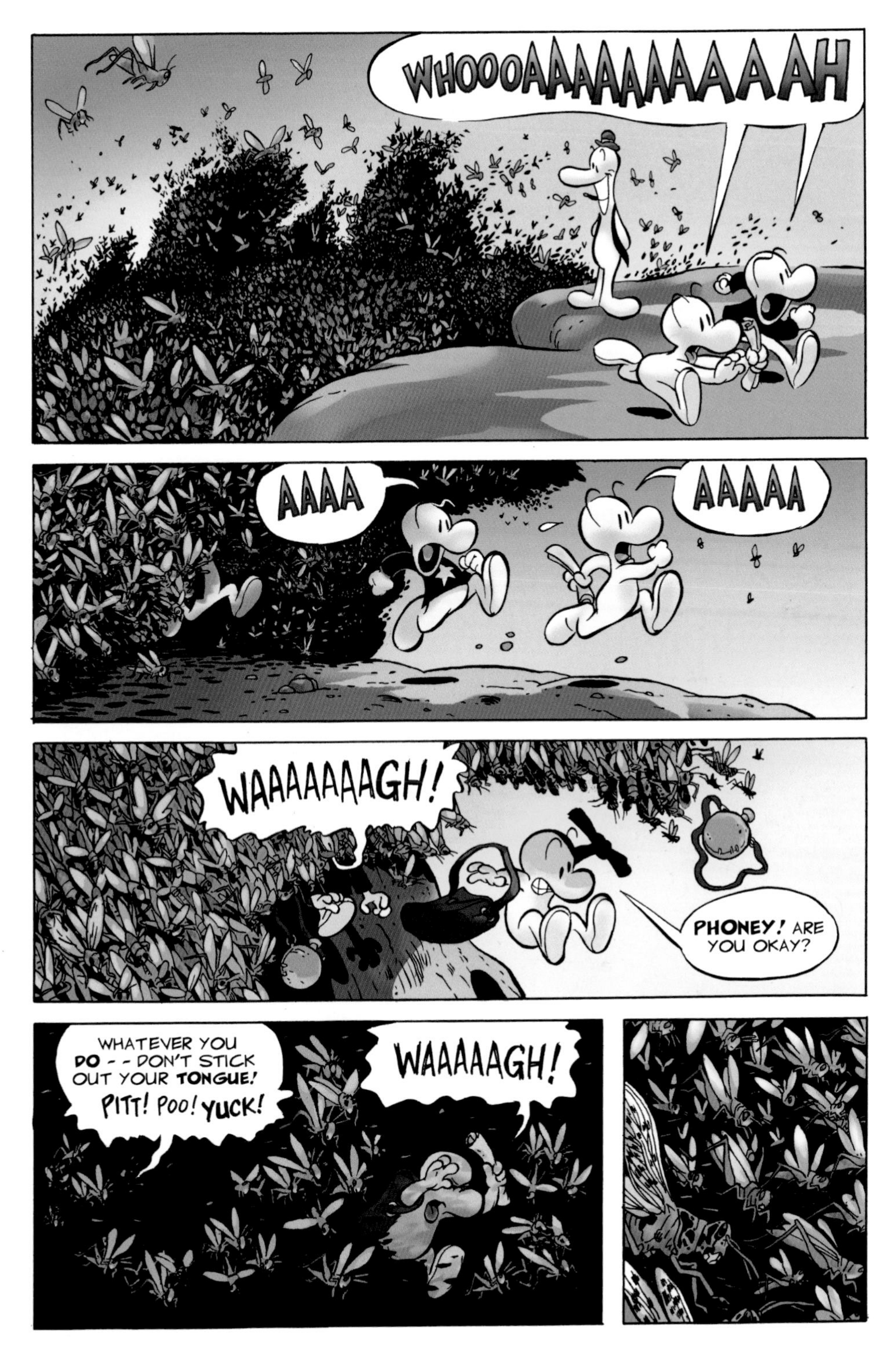
WHOOOAAAAAAAAAAH
AAAA
AAAAA
WAAAAAAAGH!
PHONEY! ARE YOU OKAY?
WHATEVER YOU DO - - DON'T STICK OUT YOUR TONGUE!
PITT! POO! YUCK!
WAAAAAGH!

PTT! PTT! PUH!

YEEEE! I CAN'T BELIEVE I WASN'T JUST KILLED!
PHONEY! SMILEY! GO BACK! DON'T COME THIS WAY! IT'S A CLIFF!
...MAYBE THEY'RE ALREADY DOWN HERE!
PHONEY BONE! SMILEY!
HEY!
HEY, GUYS! I'M DOWN IN THIS GULLEY! CAN YOU HEAR ME?!!

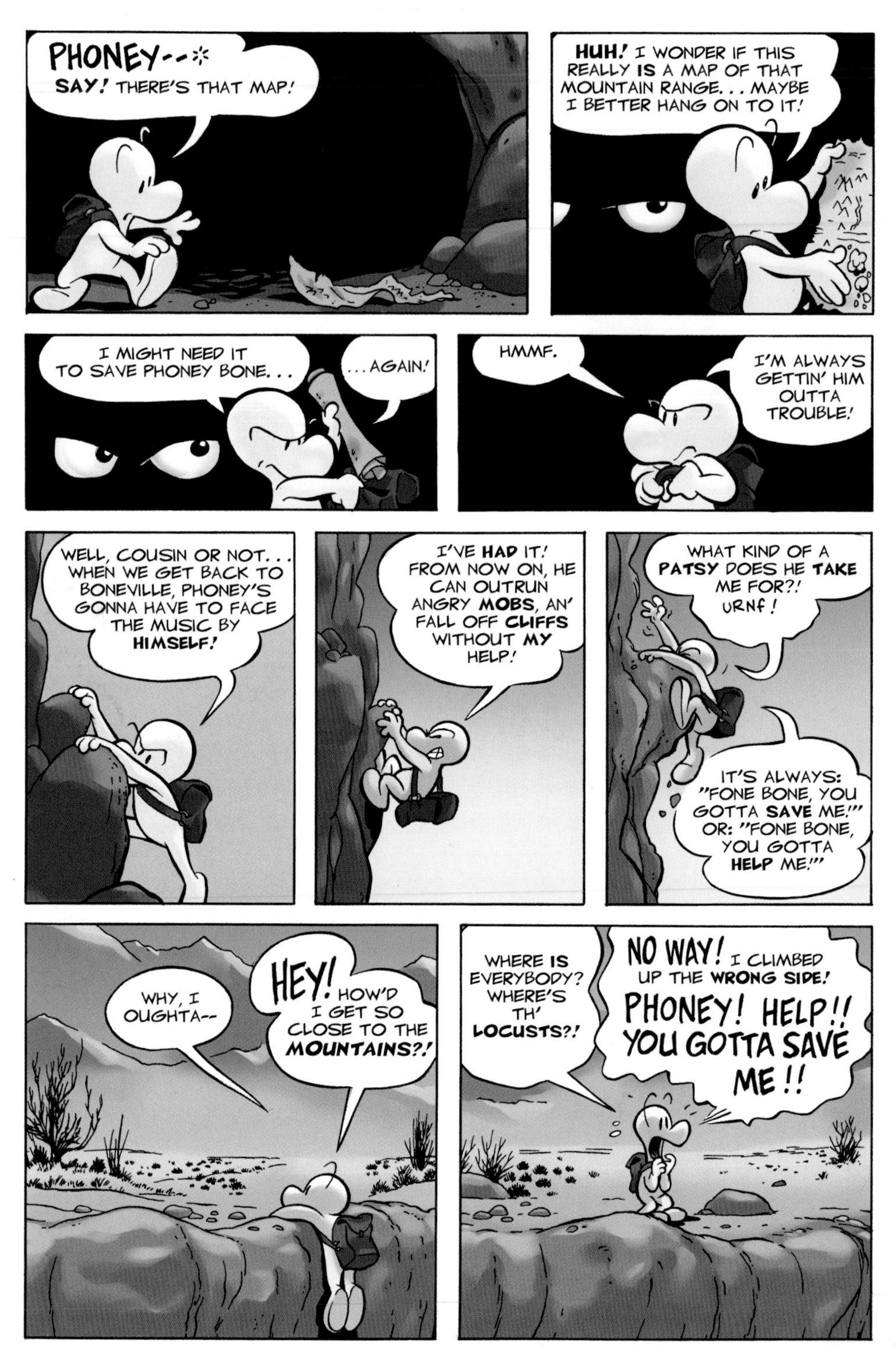
PHONEY--
SAY! THERE'S THAT MAP!
HUH! I WONDER IF THIS REALLY IS A MAP OF THAT MOUNTAIN RANGE. . . MAYBE I BETTER HANG ON TO IT!
I MIGHT NEED IT TO SAVE PHONEY BONE. . .
. . . AGAIN!
HMMF.
I'M ALWAYS GETTIN' HIM OUTTA TROUBLE!
WELL, COUSIN OR NOT. . . WHEN WE GET BACK TO BONEVILLE, PHONEY'S GONNA HAVE TO FACE THE MUSIC BY HIMSELF!
I'VE HAD IT! FROM NOW ON, HE CAN OUTRUN ANGRY MOBS, AN' FALL OFF CLIFFS WITHOUT MY HELP!
WHAT KIND OF A PATSY DOES HE TAKE ME FOR?! URNF!
IT'S ALWAYS: "FONE BONE, YOU GOTTA SAVE ME!" OR: "FONE BONE, YOU GOTTA HELP ME!"
WHY, I OUGHTA--
HEY! HOW'D I GET SO CLOSE TO THE MOUNTAINS?!
WHERE IS EVERYBODY? WHERE'S TH' LOCUSTS?!
NO WAY! I CLIMBED UP THE WRONG SIDE!
PHONEY! HELP!! YOU GOTTA SAVE ME!!

THE MAP

OH, MY GOSH! THEY'RE NOWHERE IN SIGHT!
PHONEY!
HEY!
!
A CIGAR BUTT!
ANOTHER ONE!
JEEZ... I HOPE SMILEY DOESN'T RUN OUT OF CIGARS BEFORE I CATCH UP TO HIM.

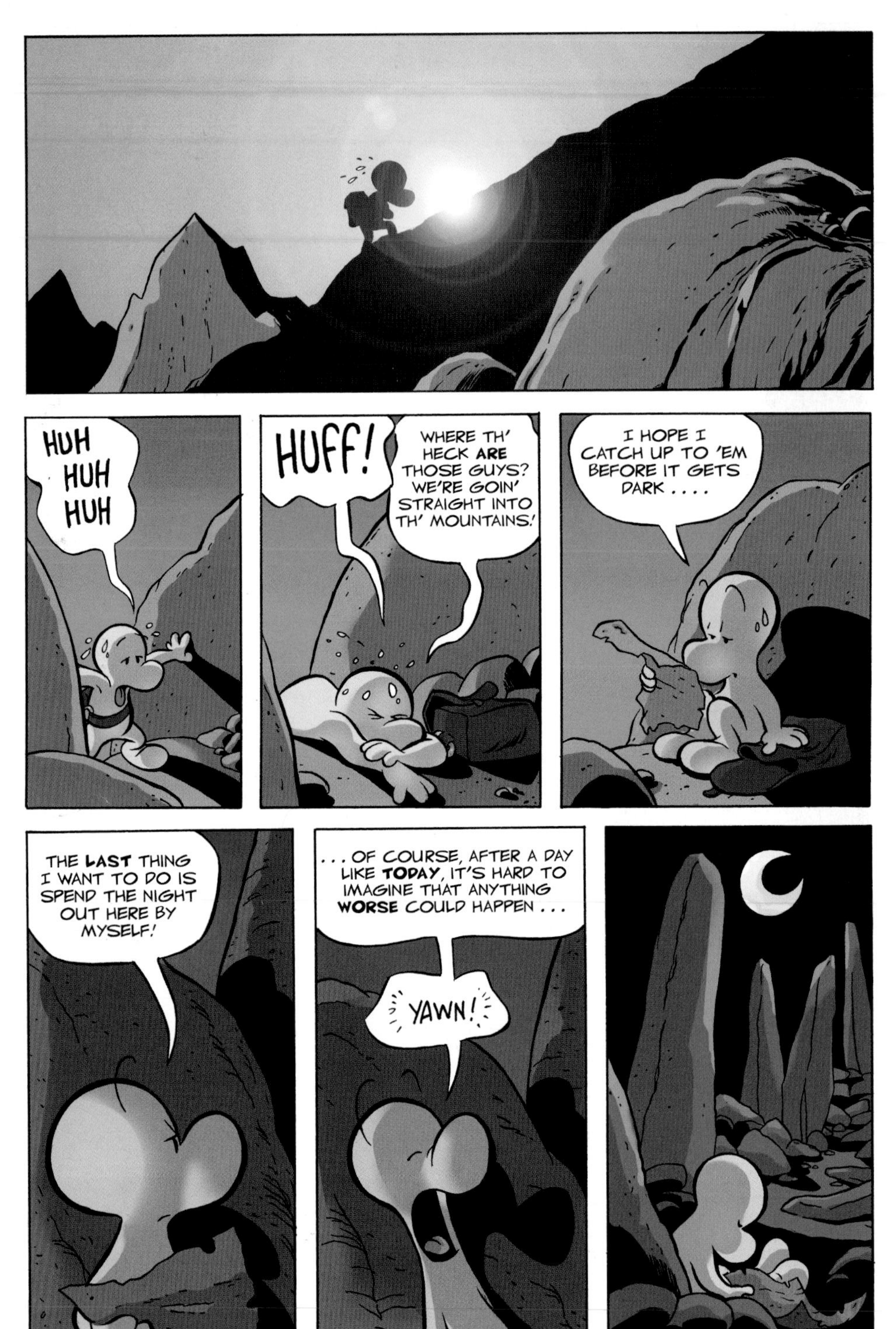
HUH
HUH
HUH
HUFF!
WHERE TH' HECK ARE THOSE GUYS? WE'RE GOIN' STRAIGHT INTO TH' MOUNTAINS!
I HOPE I CATCH UP TO 'EM BEFORE IT GETS DARK . . . .
THE LAST THING I WANT TO DO IS SPEND THE NIGHT OUT HERE BY MYSELF!
. . . OF COURSE, AFTER A DAY LIKE TODAY, IT'S HARD TO IMAGINE THAT ANYTHING WORSE COULD HAPPEN . . .
YAWN!

LIGHT THE TORCH...
...IS IT HIM?... IS IT THE ONE WE SEEK?
...I CANNOT TELL... LOOK FOR THE STAR ON ITS CHEST...
...NO STAR... THIS ISN'T THE ONE....
....NO... IT IS NOT HE..... ...VERY WELL.... KILL IT.... IT WILL BE OUR SUPPER....
WHO'S GONNA BE YOUR SUPPER?
GO AWAY!
DO NOT MEDDLE IN AFFAIRS THAT ARE TOO BIG FOR YOU, BOY!
WHO YOU CALLIN' BOY?
AIEEEEEEEEE! THE GREAT RED DRAGON!!

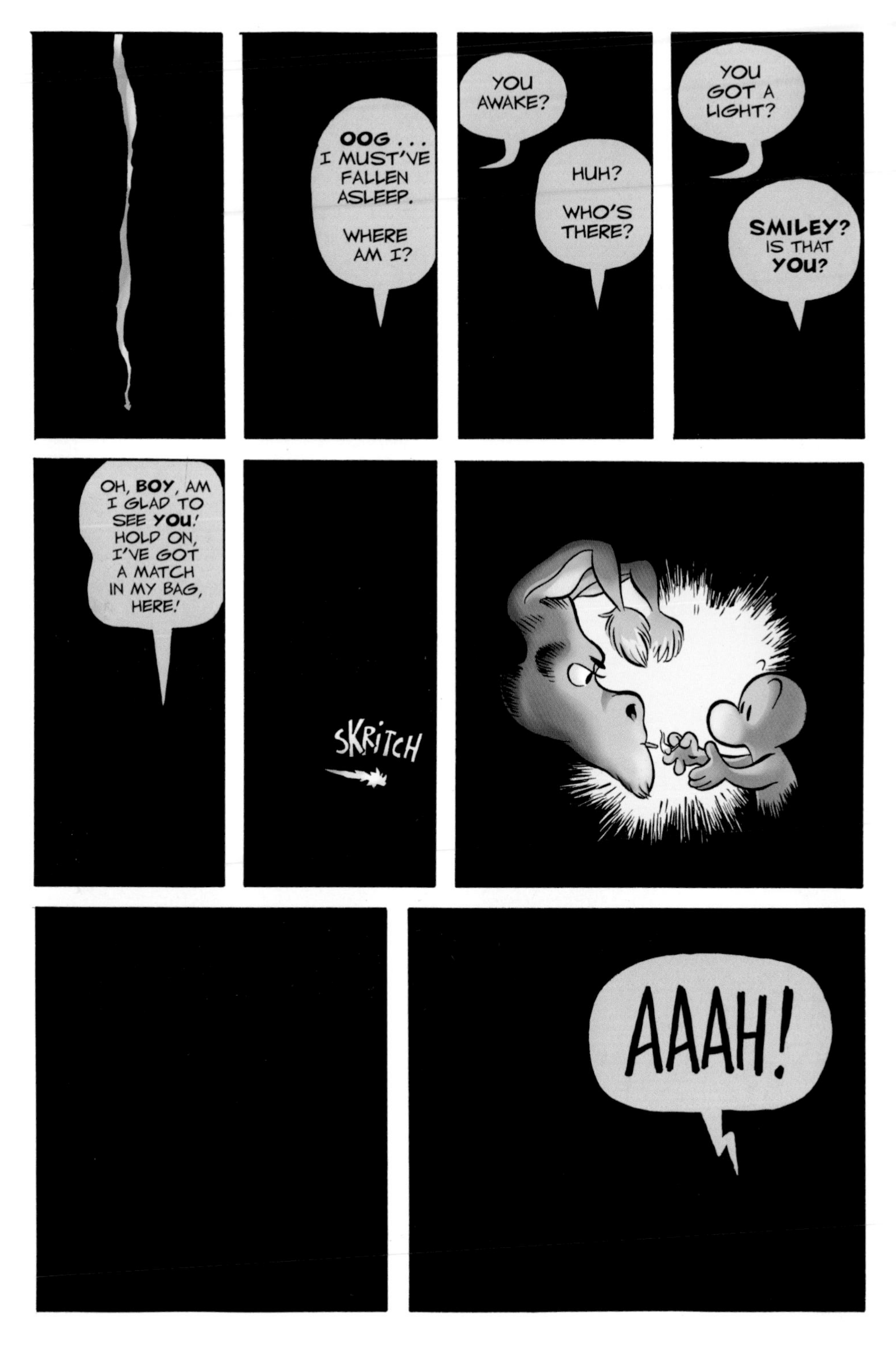
OOG . . . I MUST'VE FALLEN ASLEEP.
WHERE AM I?
YOU AWAKE?
HUH?
WHO'S THERE?
YOU GOT A LIGHT?
SMILEY? IS THAT YOU?
OH, BOY, AM I GLAD TO SEE YOU! HOLD ON, I'VE GOT A MATCH IN MY BAG, HERE!
SKRITCH
AAAH!

THANKS FOR TH' LIGHT.
DON'T MENTION IT!
SKRITCH
HELLO?
HELLO?
OH, MAN! I GOTTA QUIT GOIN' TO SLEEP ON AN EMPTY STOMACH!

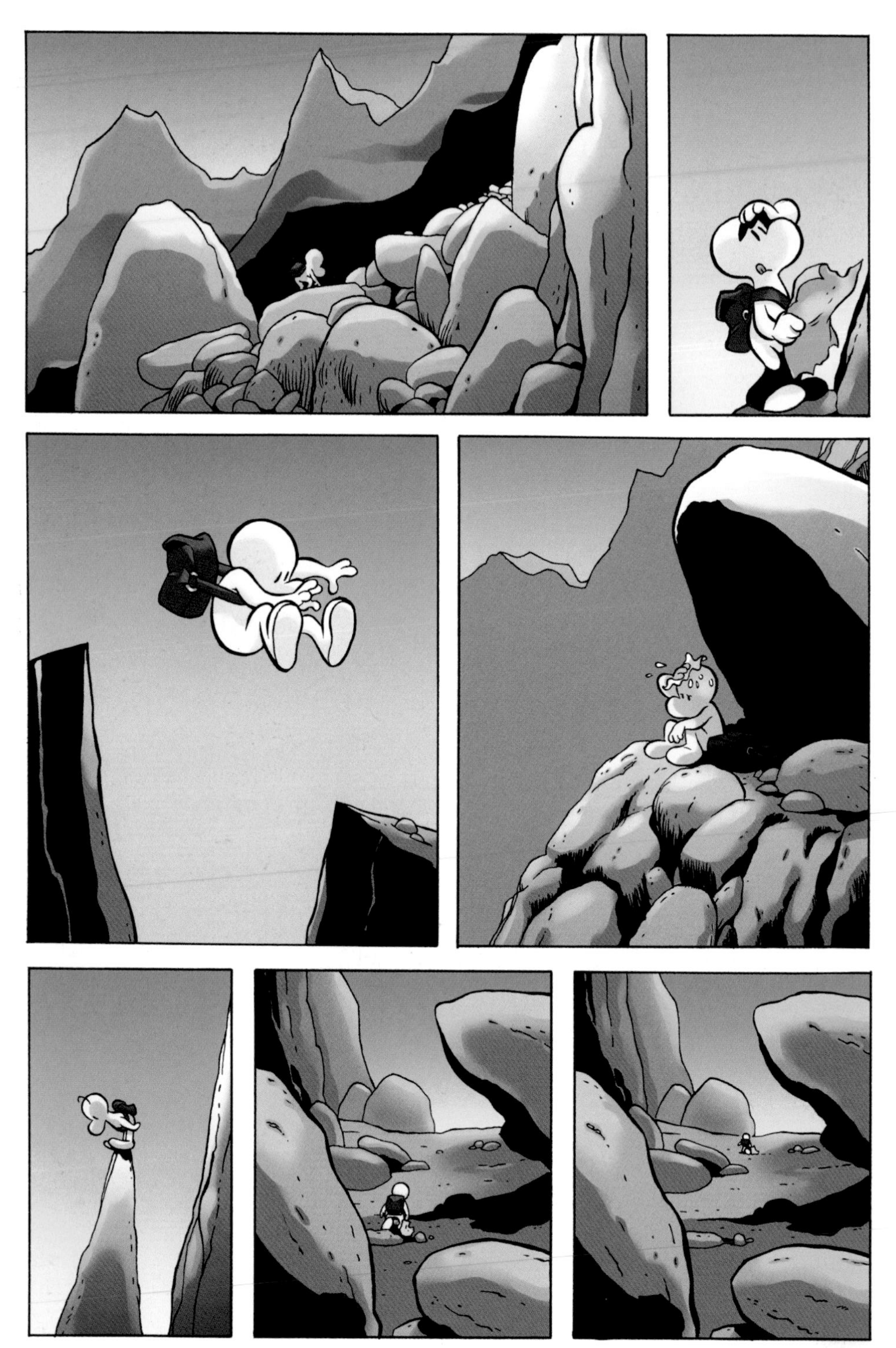

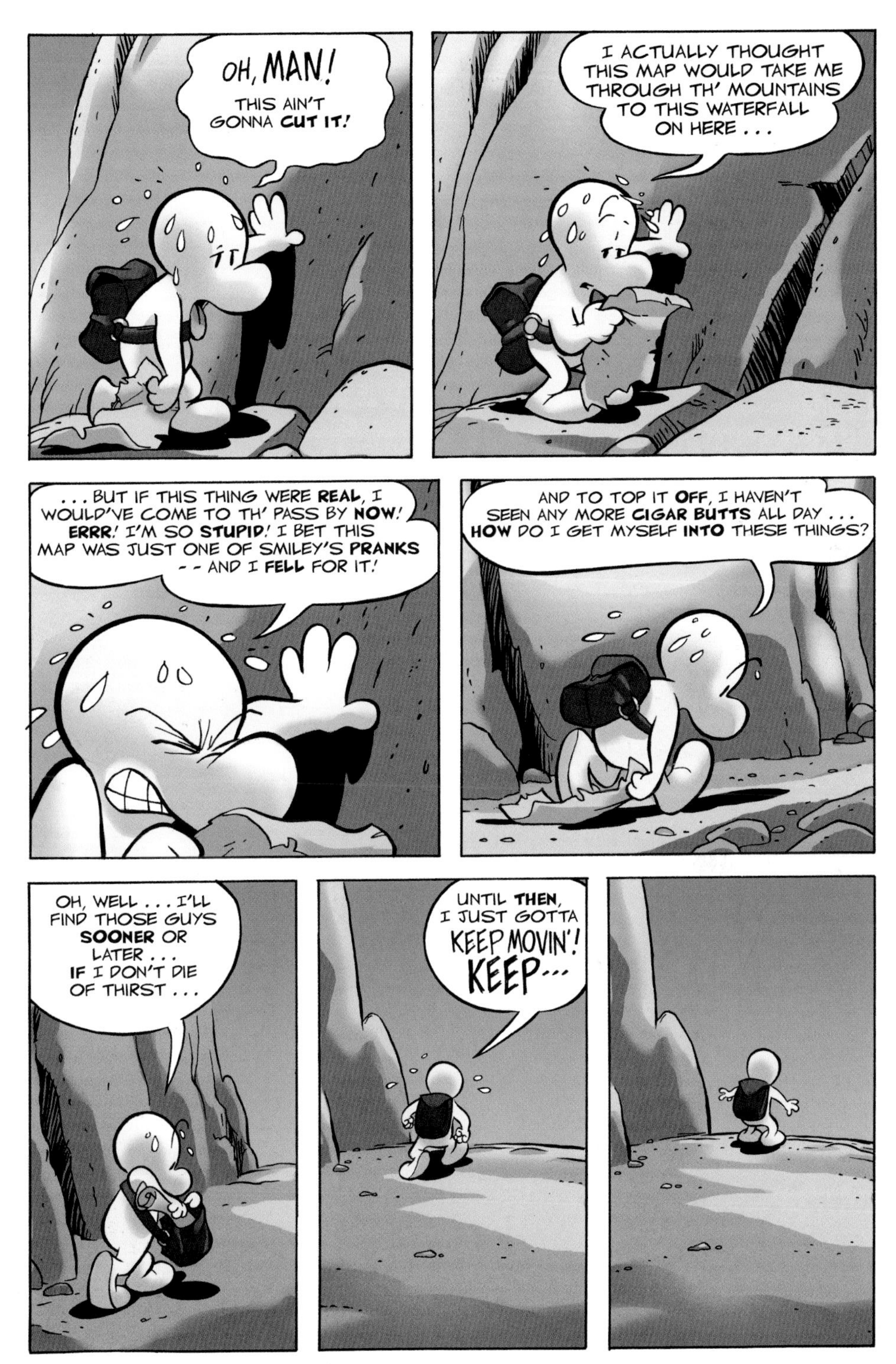
OH, MAN! THIS AIN'T GONNA CUT IT!
I ACTUALLY THOUGHT THIS MAP WOULD TAKE ME THROUGH TH' MOUNTAINS TO THIS WATERFALL ON HERE . . .
. . . BUT IF THIS THING WERE REAL, I WOULD'VE COME TO TH' PASS BY NOW! ERRR! I'M SO STUPID! I BET THIS MAP WAS JUST ONE OF SMILEY'S PRANKS - - AND I FELL FOR IT!
AND TO TOP IT OFF, I HAVEN'T SEEN ANY MORE CIGAR BUTTS ALL DAY . . . HOW DO I GET MYSELF INTO THESE THINGS?
OH, WELL . . . I'LL FIND THOSE GUYS SOONER OR LATER . . . IF I DON'T DIE OF THIRST . . .
UNTIL THEN, I JUST GOTTA KEEP MOVIN'! KEEP...

COOL.
I MADE IT!
THAT STUPID MAP WAS RIGHT! YESSIREE, BOB! THERE'S WATER ON TH' MENU TONIGHT!
I COULD KISS SMILEY BONE FOR FINDING THAT MAP!
I MIGHT EVEN KISS PHONEY RIGHT BEFORE I STRANGLE HIM!

AND LOOK! ONE OF SMILEY'S CIGAR STUBS!
HEY! WATCH IT! YOU ALMOST STEPPED ON ME!
WHOOPS! HELLO! WHAT ARE YOU SUPPOSED TO BE?
I'M TED! I'M A BUG!
YOU LOOK MORE LIKE A LEAF!
A LEAF?! THAT'S A INSULT! WHERE'S MY BIG BROTHER?
HEY, HOLD ON! I DIDN'T MEAN ANY HARM! BESIDES, WHAT COULD YOUR BIG BROTHER DO TO ME?
WHOA.
IS YOU PICKIN' ON TED?
I - - JUST SAID HE LOOKS LIKE A LEAF!
WHAT ARE YOU? A TROUBLE-MAKER? WE DON'T NEED YOUR KIND IN OUR VALLEY!
I GUESS HE DIDN'T MEAN NO HARM, BIG BROTHER! YOU DON'T HAS TO HIT HIM IF YOU DON'T WANT!
LISTEN TO HIM! LISTEN TO HIM!
WELL, OKAY, TED, IF YOU SAY SO . . . .
I'M NOT TRYIN' TO CAUSE TROUBLE! I'M LOOKING FOR MY COUSINS! WE GOT SEPARATED, AN' NOW I'M LOST! YOU WOULDN'T KNOW HOW TO GET TO BONEVILLE FROM HERE, WOULD YA?
BONEVILLE? NEVER HEARD OF IT . . .

BUT YOU BETTER FIND IT - - FAST! IT'S AUTUMN NOW, AN' WINTER STRIKES QUICK IN THESE PARTS . . . AN' WHEN IT DOES, NOBODY CAN GET THROUGH THOSE MOUNTAINS . . .
. . . IN OR OUT!
SO I SUGGEST YOU MAKE YOUR VISIT HERE A SHORT ONE, OR YOU'LL BE STUCK FOR TH' WINTER. AN' I DON'T THINK YOU WANNA DO THAT!
NO.
DEFINITELY NOT.
GOOD. I'LL LET YA GO FOR NOW, SINCE TED SEEMS TO LIKE YA OKAY... BUT DON'T FERGET!
NO DAWDLIN'!
THANK YOU FOR NOT HITTING ME.
DON'T WORRY 'BOUT HIM. . . HE'S ACTUAL A REAL NICE GUY!
WELL . . . NOW WE GOTTA FIGGER OUT WHAT TA DO WITH YA . . . SAY! I KNOW! I'LL TAKE YA TO SEE THORN! C'MON! WHAT'S YER NAME, MISTER?
FONE BONE. SO WHO'S THIS THORN? HE'S NOT ANOTHER BIG BUG, IS HE?
HO, HO! NO!
THORN KNOWS JES' ABOUT EVER'THIN' IN TH' WHOLE WORLD!
BUT, LISTEN, BONE! BIG BROTHER WAS RIGHT ABOUT WINTER! SHE HITS FAST! 'N' IF YOU WANTS TA GIT HOME, YOU GOTTA DO IT BEFORE SHE SNOWS!
DON'T WORRY! I'M JUST GONNA FIND MY COUSINS, AN' THEN I'M OUTTA HERE!

WHERE CAN I GET SOMETHING TO DRINK? I'M DYIN' OF THIRST!
WE CAN STOP BY TH' BARRELHAVEN! THEY BREWS TH' BEST STUFF AROUN'!
eh?
COMRADE! WE ARE ABOUT TO FEAST! QUICK! GET YOUR FAT CARCASS BEHIND THIS BUSH AND GET READY!
HELLO, SMALL MAMMAL.... COULD YOU STEP IN HERE FOR A MOMENT? I'VE GOT SOMETHING TO SHOW YOU....
CAN'T YOU SHOW ME OUT HERE, WHERE I'VE GOT RUNNIN' SPACE?
NO! NO! PLEASE! STEP IN HERE -- YOUR FRIEND THE DRAGON ISN'T AROUND, IS HE?
HEY, TED! WHERE YOU GOIN'?
YOU'RE ON YER OWN, BONE!
QUICK, COMRADE! START THE COOKING FIRE!
NO. YOU CALLED ME FAT.

TED! WAIT FOR ME!
WELL, WELL... LOOK WHO'S JOINED US FOR SUPPER... GO START THE COOKING FIRE!!
NO. YOU CALLED ME FAT.
NO?!! WHAT DO YOU MEAN NO?!!
AND IT'S NOT THE FIRST TIME YOU'VE DONE IT, EITHER...
COMRADE... BE REASONABLE! I WASN'T THINKING--- I WAS TRYING TO CATCH OUR DINNER--- THIS ISN'T THE TIME---
I TAKE IT BACK.... YOU'RE NOT FAT.
TOO LATE!
PLEASE, COMRADE! I JUST WANT TO CHOP HIM UP FOR THE STEW!
AND THAT'S ANOTHER THING! I'M TIRED OF STEW! I WANT TO PUT HIM IN A CRUST AND BAKE A LIGHT FLUFFY QUICHE!
QUICHE?! WHAT KIND OF FOOD IS THAT FOR A MONSTER TO EAT?!...... LISTEN, DO YOU THINK YOU COULD COME BACK IN HALF AN HOUR? WE'LL HAVE THIS STRAIGHTENED OUT BY THEN!
WHY DIDN'T YOU STOP ME?
WHY SHOULD I? YOU'RE SO SMART!

TED!
C'MON, TED! WHERE ARE YOU? YOU GOTTA TAKE ME TO SEE THORN!
-- I'M SORRY I CALLED YOU A LEAF!
WHOOOOOP! WATER! I HEAR WATER!!
WATER!
WATER! WATER!
WATER! MMMM WATER! WATER! MMMM WATER! WATER! MMMMMM MM MM OH, MAN!
WHAT AM I GONNA DO? WHAT IF I CAN'T FIND MY COUSINS BEFORE IT SNOWS? WE COULD BE TRAPPED HERE FOR TH' WHOLE WINTER!
I GOTTA GET OUTTA HERE! THIS FOREST IS TOO WEIRD FOR ME!
RUMMMMBLE

WHUMP!
CASE IN POINT.

BONE™
CRACK!
PERFECT! NOW ALL I NEED IS ONE MORE GOOD-SIZED STICK, AND I'LL HAVE ENOUGH!
♫
OH, BONE! MISTER BONE! YOO-HOO!

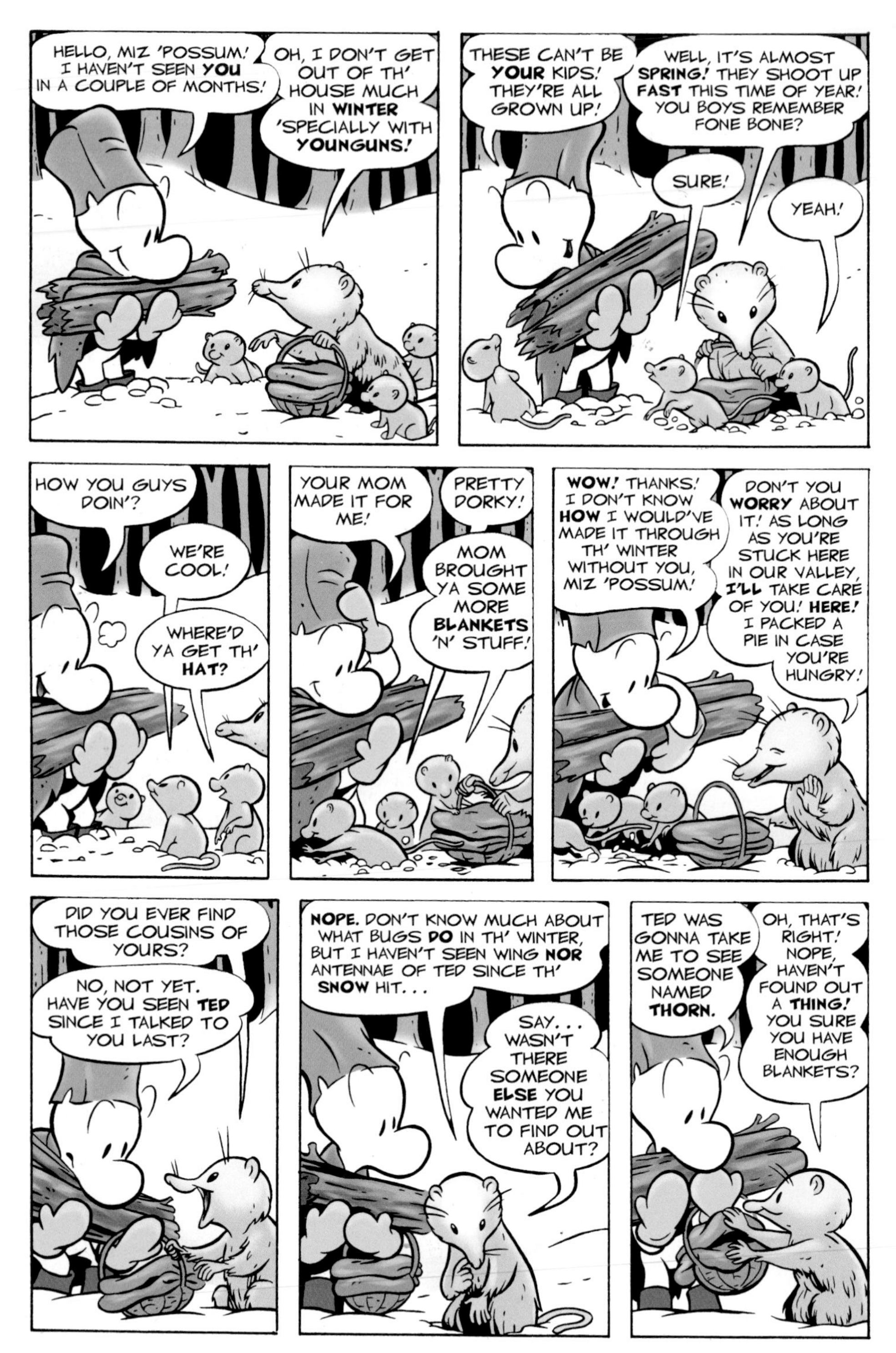
HELLO, MIZ 'POSSUM! I HAVEN'T SEEN YOU IN A COUPLE OF MONTHS!
OH, I DON'T GET OUT OF TH' HOUSE MUCH IN WINTER 'SPECIALLY WITH YOUNGUNS!
THESE CAN'T BE YOUR KIDS! THEY'RE ALL GROWN UP!
WELL, IT'S ALMOST SPRING! THEY SHOOT UP FAST THIS TIME OF YEAR! YOU BOYS REMEMBER FONE BONE?
SURE!
YEAH!
HOW YOU GUYS DOIN'?
WE'RE COOL!
WHERE'D YA GET TH' HAT?
YOUR MOM MADE IT FOR ME!
PRETTY DORKY!
MOM BROUGHT YA SOME MORE BLANKETS 'N' STUFF!
WOW! THANKS! I DON'T KNOW HOW I WOULD'VE MADE IT THROUGH TH' WINTER WITHOUT YOU, MIZ 'POSSUM!
DON'T YOU WORRY ABOUT IT! AS LONG AS YOU'RE STUCK HERE IN OUR VALLEY, I'LL TAKE CARE OF YOU! HERE! I PACKED A PIE IN CASE YOU'RE HUNGRY!
DID YOU EVER FIND THOSE COUSINS OF YOURS?
NO, NOT YET. HAVE YOU SEEN TED SINCE I TALKED TO YOU LAST?
NOPE. DON'T KNOW MUCH ABOUT WHAT BUGS DO IN TH' WINTER, BUT I HAVEN'T SEEN WING NOR ANTENNAE OF TED SINCE TH' SNOW HIT. . .
SAY. . . WASN'T THERE SOMEONE ELSE YOU WANTED ME TO FIND OUT ABOUT?
TED WAS GONNA TAKE ME TO SEE SOMEONE NAMED THORN.
OH, THAT'S RIGHT! NOPE, HAVEN'T FOUND OUT A THING! YOU SURE YOU HAVE ENOUGH BLANKETS?

YES, MA'M. SIGH. WELL, THANKS ANYWAY, MIZ 'POSSUM! IF THERE'S EVER ANYTHING I CAN DO --
AS A MATTER OF FACT, I'M ON MY WAY OVER TO MIZ HEDGEHOG'S PLACE, 'N' I WAS WONDERIN' IF YOU'D MIND WATCHIN' TH' KIDS?
ALL RIGHT! WE'RE GONNA STAY WITH FONE BONE!
ME?! BUT. . . I DON'T KNOW ANYTHING ABOUT BABY 'POSSUMS!
IT'LL JUST BE FOR AN HOUR OR TWO! YOU BOYS BE GOOD NOW!
DON'T WORRY ABOUT US, MOM!
WELL . . . C'MON, GUYS. YOU CAN HELP ME PUT THE FINISHING TOUCH ON MY HOUSE!
RUN INSIDE WHERE IT'S WARM . . . I'LL JUST BE A SECOND!
WHOOP!
YIPPEE!
THERE WE GO! COZY AS AN IGLOO! BY THE TIME THIS MELTS, IT'LL BE SPRING, AN' THEN I'M OUTTA HERE!
SMASH! CRASH!
HEY, GUYS! TAKE IT EASY IN TH--
CRUNCH

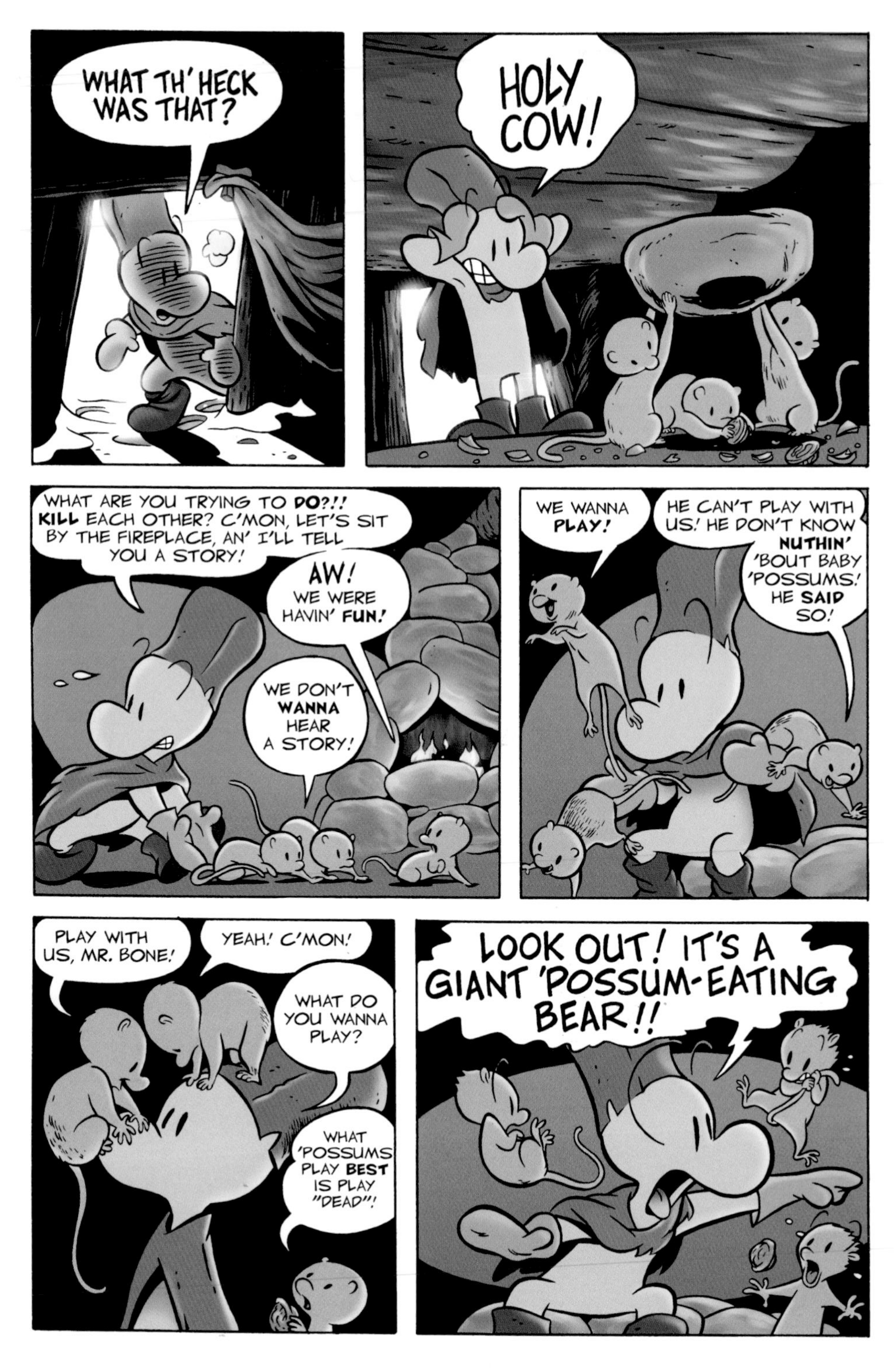
WHAT TH' HECK WAS THAT?
HOLY COW!
WHAT ARE YOU TRYING TO DO?!! KILL EACH OTHER? C'MON, LET'S SIT BY THE FIREPLACE, AN' I'LL TELL YOU A STORY!
AW! WE WERE HAVIN' FUN!
WE DON'T WANNA HEAR A STORY!
WE WANNA PLAY!
HE CAN'T PLAY WITH US! HE DON'T KNOW NUTHIN' 'BOUT BABY 'POSSUMS! HE SAID SO!
PLAY WITH US, MR. BONE!
YEAH! C'MON!
WHAT DO YOU WANNA PLAY?
WHAT 'POSSUMS PLAY BEST IS PLAY "DEAD"!
LOOK OUT! IT'S A GIANT 'POSSUM-EATING BEAR!!

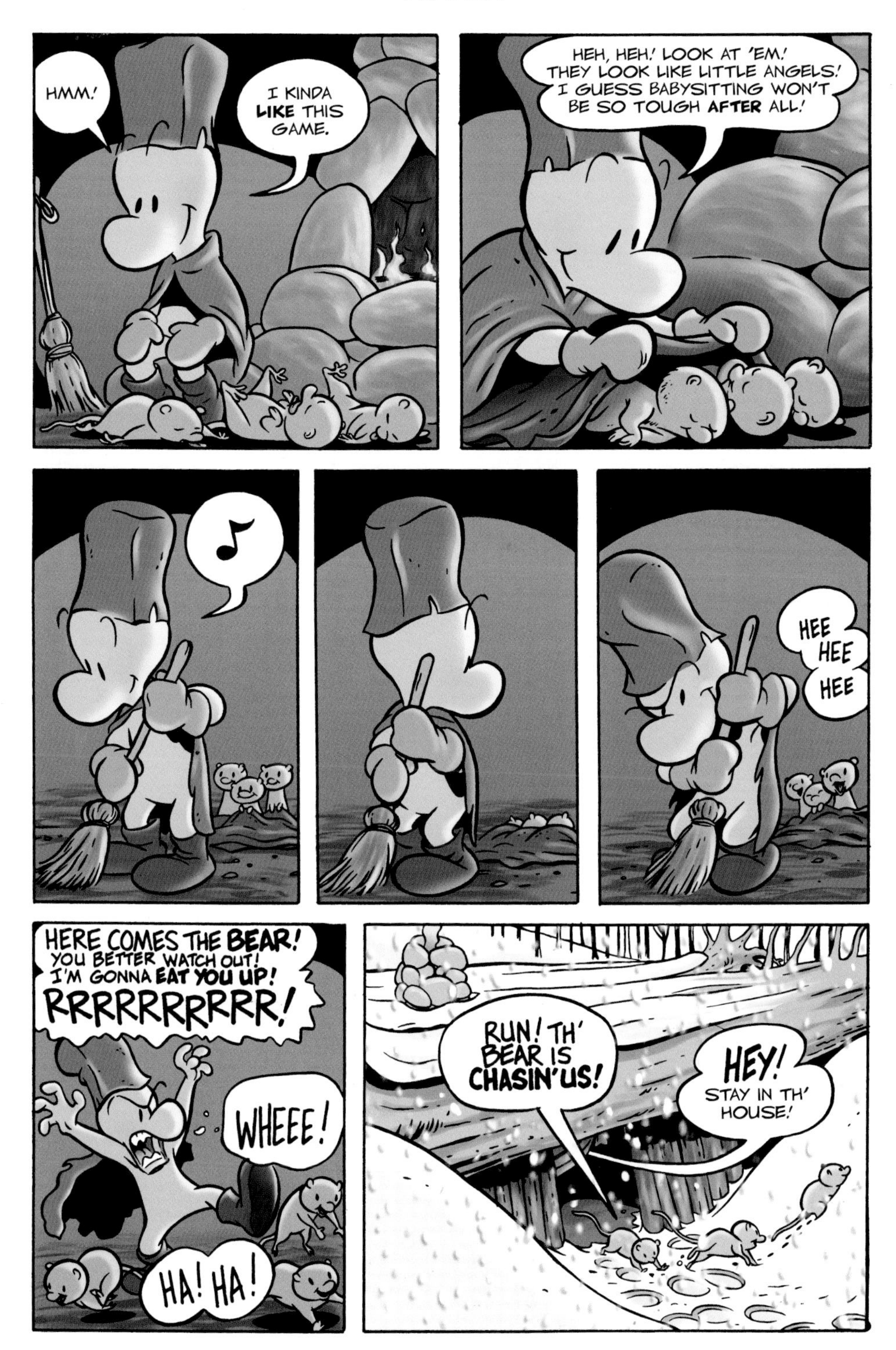
HMM!
I KINDA LIKE THIS GAME.
HEH, HEH! LOOK AT 'EM! THEY LOOK LIKE LITTLE ANGELS! I GUESS BABYSITTING WON'T BE SO TOUGH AFTER ALL!
♪
HEE HEE HEE
HERE COMES THE BEAR! YOU BETTER WATCH OUT! I'M GONNA EAT YOU UP! RRRRRRRRR!
WHEEE!
HA! HA!
RUN! TH' BEAR IS CHASIN' US!
HEY! STAY IN TH' HOUSE!

COME BACK HERE!
CATCH US IF YOU CAN!
HA! HA!
I'M SERIOUS! QUIT FOOLIN' AROUND!
BOYS?
ALL RIGHT.... THEY WANT ME TO CATCH 'EM ... I'LL CATCH 'EM!
AHA! HIDING IN TH' BUSHES ARE YOU?!! WELL, MR. BEAR IS GETTING HUNGRY!!
RRRRR-R-R! NOW I'M GOING TO---
WHOOOOOPS!

HI, FELLAS. LONG TIME NO SEE!
SSSSSSSSSSSS
YOU DON'T SAY! WELL, NICE TALKIN' WITH YA! THANKS FOR WATCHIN' TH' KIDS! GOTTA GO!
AARRAAARRAAR
QUICK! YOU KIDS RUN HOME! I'LL SLOW 'EM DOWN!
HELP! MOMMA!
THE RAT CREATURES ARE AFTER US!!
OW!OW! OOOOOH! MY ANKLE!
AARRARR

MAN! WHAT TH' HECK DID YOU EAT FOR LUNCH?!
!
THAT LITTLE DEAD THING WE FOUND UNDER A BUSH ... YOU HAD SOME, DIDN'T YOU?
YES. IT WAS QUITE GOOD.
HEY! WHERE'D HE GO?

THOSE RAT CREATURES WOULD HAVE TO BE PRETTY STUPID TO FOLLOW ME ON TO THIS FRAIL, LITTLE BRANCH!
STUPID, STUPID RAT CREATURES!!

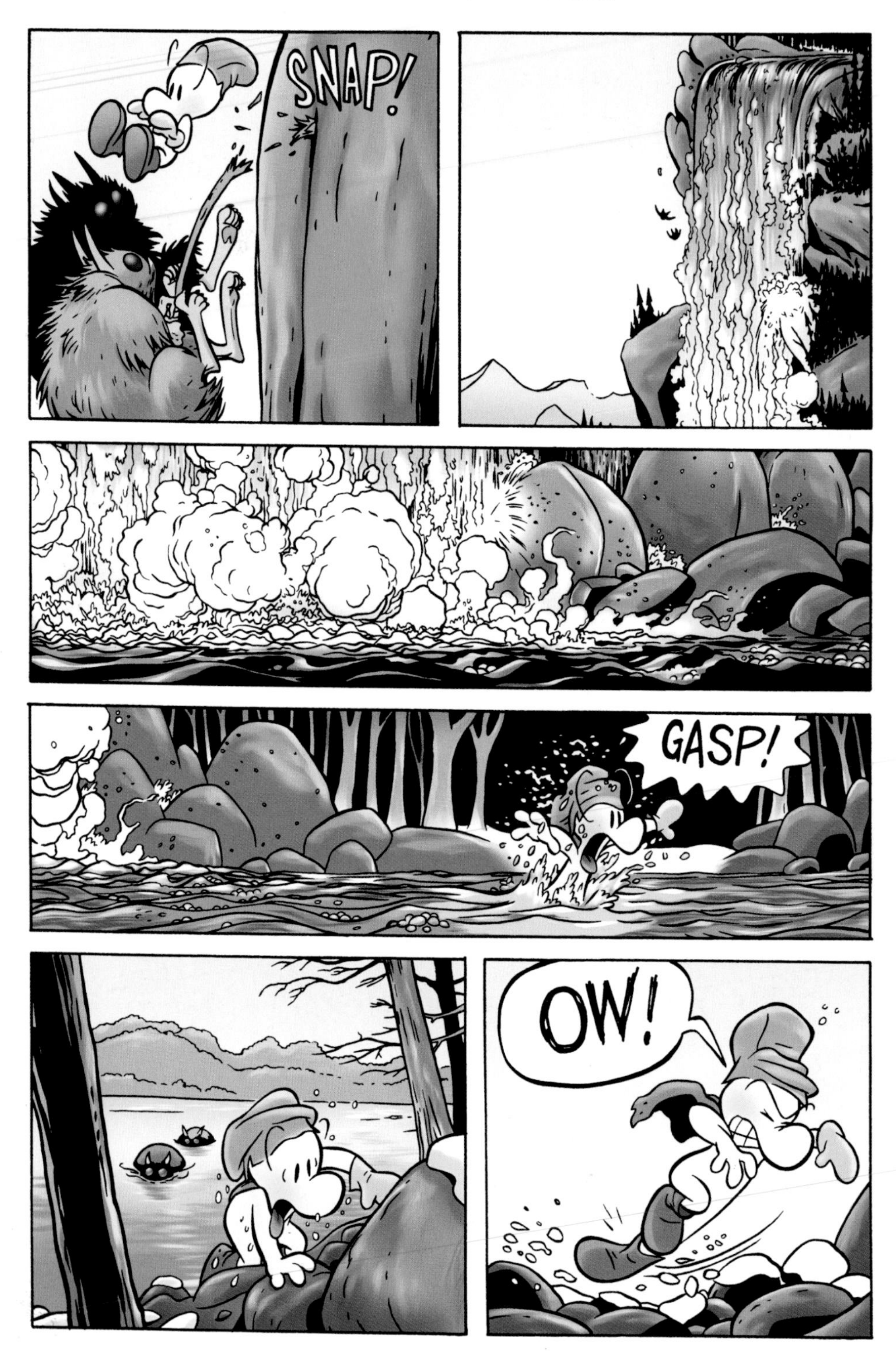
SNAP!
GASP!
OW!

YIKES!
THIS TIME I REALLY DID HURT MY ANKLE!
WHAT A SHAME.
WHAT DO YOU SAY, COMRADE? SHALL WE HAVE A NICE, HOT STEW? OR SHOULD WE EAT HIM RAW?
MMMMM, MM! I SAY WE BAKE HIM IN A QUICHE!
YOU KNOW HOW MUCH I LIKE QUI--
SEEMS TO ME YOU BOYS HAVE A SHORT MEMORY!
SSSSSSSSS!
THE DRAGON!
WE WEREN'T GOING TO EAT HIM, DRAGON-- WE WERE ONLY PLAYING WITH HIM!
BEAT IT!
YIPE! YIPE! YIPE!
HEY!
WHAT ARE YOU DOING? DON'T LET 'EM GET AWAY!

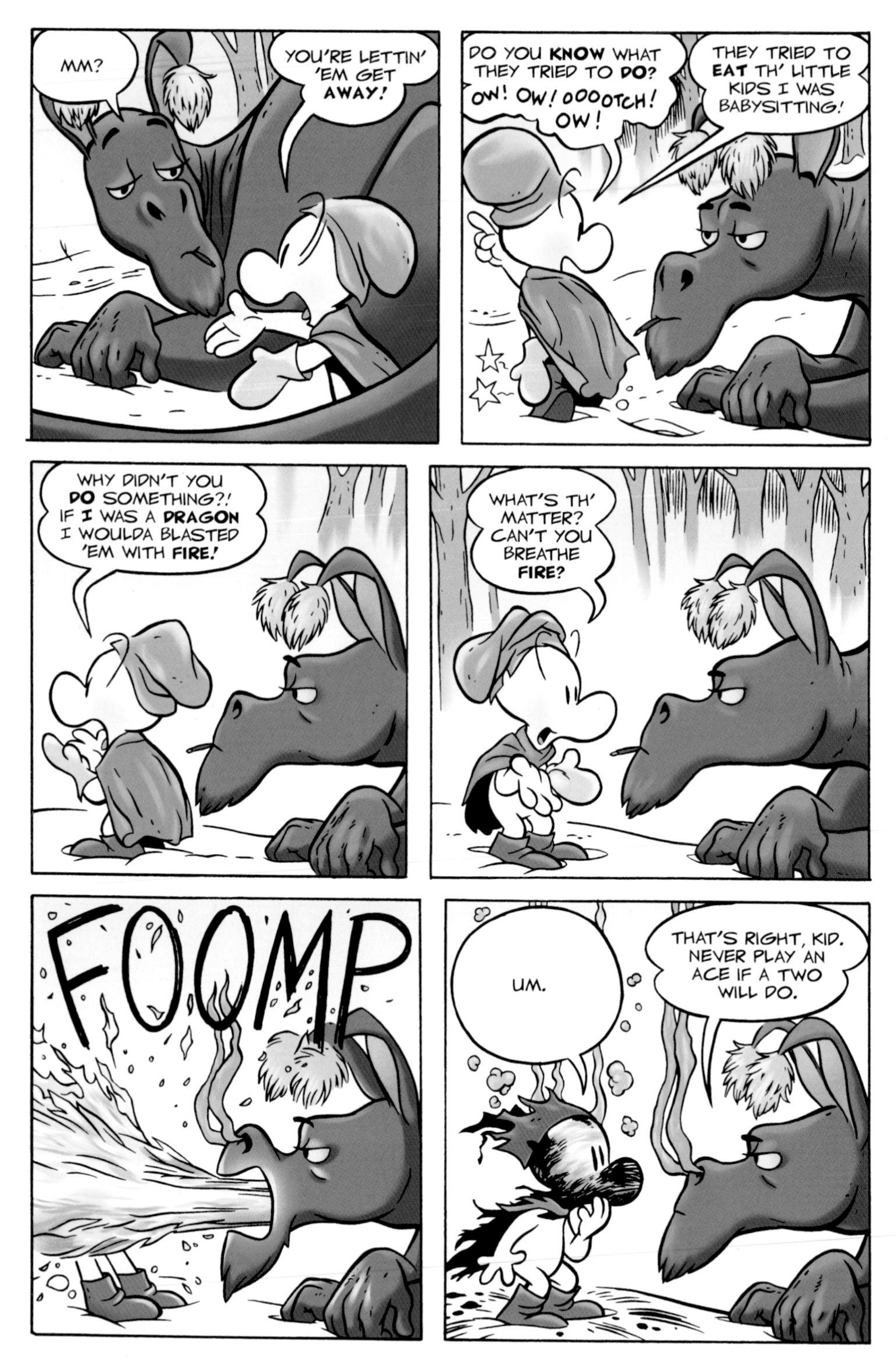
MM?
YOU'RE LETTIN' 'EM GET AWAY!
DO YOU KNOW WHAT THEY TRIED TO DO?
OW! OW! OOOOTCH! OW!
THEY TRIED TO EAT TH' LITTLE KIDS I WAS BABYSITTING!
WHY DIDN'T YOU DO SOMETHING?! IF I WAS A DRAGON I WOULDA BLASTED 'EM WITH FIRE!
WHAT'S TH' MATTER? CAN'T YOU BREATHE FIRE?
FOOMP
UM.
THAT'S RIGHT, KID. NEVER PLAY AN ACE IF A TWO WILL DO.

UH . . . WELL . . . IT WAS NICE MEETING YOU, BUT I BETTER GO FIND TH' KIDS!
WHOA.
DON'T WORRY ABOUT THE KIDS. THEY'RE SAFE.
GO STRAIGHT DOWN THE HILL. IT'S A SHORTCUT TO MIZ 'POSSUM'S HOUSE.
. . . UH . . . SURE!
THANKS!
!
HEY! HOW'D YOU KNOW I WAS LOOKING FOR MIZ 'POSSUM'S KIDS?!
BONE!

BONE! THERE YOU ARE! WE CAME AS FAST AS WE COULD! ARE YOU ALL RIGHT?
YAY!
HE'S SAFE!
I'M OKAY. . . I HAD A LITTLE RUN-IN WITH A DRAGON, BUT THE IMPORTANT THING IS THAT WE'RE ALL SAFE!
A DRAGON? REALLY?
GET OUTTA TOWN!
SEE HOW HE IS WITH TH' KIDS? HE'S ALWAYS GOT A STORY!
IT'S NOT ENOUGH THAT HE CHASED OFF THOSE BULLIES. . . NOW HE'S TURNED IT INTO A YARN WITH A DRAGON IN IT!
ISN'T THAT PRECIOUS?
WHAT WAS THAT?
OH! I'M SORRY, BONE! TEE HEE! GO AHEAD AN' TELL TH' BOYS ABOUT TH' FEROCIOUS FIRE-BREATHING DRAGON!
YEAH! TELL US! WERE YOU SCARED?
OF COURSE I WAS!
HE'S SO MODEST!
AND BRAVE!
WHAT HAPPENED, FONE BONE? DID YOU KILL TH' DRAGON?
WHAT HAPPENED TO YOUR HAT? DID THE DRAGON DO IT?
HE'S PULLIN' OUR TAILS! EVERYBODY KNOWS DRAGONS ARE MAKE-BELIEVE!
AREN'T THEY?!
THAT'S ENOUGH QUESTIONS FOR NOW. UNCLE BONE MUST BE VERY TIRED. LET'S ALL GO HOME WHERE IT'S WARM AND SAFE, AND THEN BONE CAN TELL US ALL ABOUT HIS ADVENTURE!
MAYBE HE'D LIKE TO STOP AND CLEAN UP FIRST.

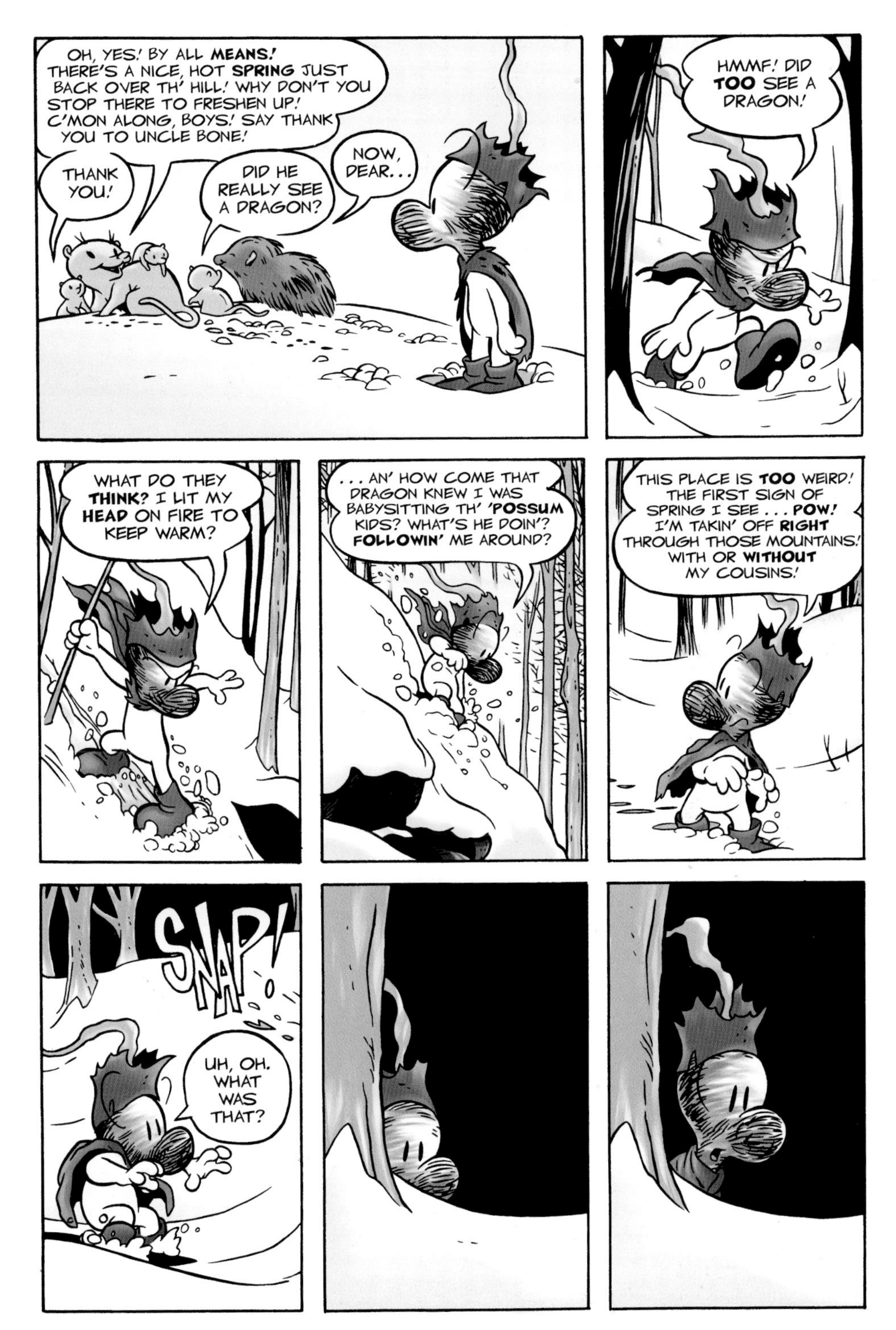
OH, YES! BY ALL MEANS! THERE'S A NICE, HOT SPRING JUST BACK OVER TH' HILL! WHY DON'T YOU STOP THERE TO FRESHEN UP! C'MON ALONG, BOYS! SAY THANK YOU TO UNCLE BONE!
THANK YOU!
DID HE REALLY SEE A DRAGON?
NOW, DEAR...
HMMF! DID TOO SEE A DRAGON!
WHAT DO THEY THINK? I LIT MY HEAD ON FIRE TO KEEP WARM?
...AN' HOW COME THAT DRAGON KNEW I WAS BABYSITTING TH' 'POSSUM KIDS? WHAT'S HE DOIN'? FOLLOWIN' ME AROUND?
THIS PLACE IS TOO WEIRD! THE FIRST SIGN OF SPRING I SEE... POW! I'M TAKIN' OFF RIGHT THROUGH THOSE MOUNTAINS! WITH OR WITHOUT MY COUSINS!
SNAP!
UH, OH. WHAT WAS THAT?

♪ MMMMMM ♪

FOOM!

OW! OW!
SSSSSSSSSSS
WHAT HAPPENED?
DON'T BE AFRAID! I WON'T HURT YOU!
C'MON DOWN! WE'LL SHARE THE POOL!

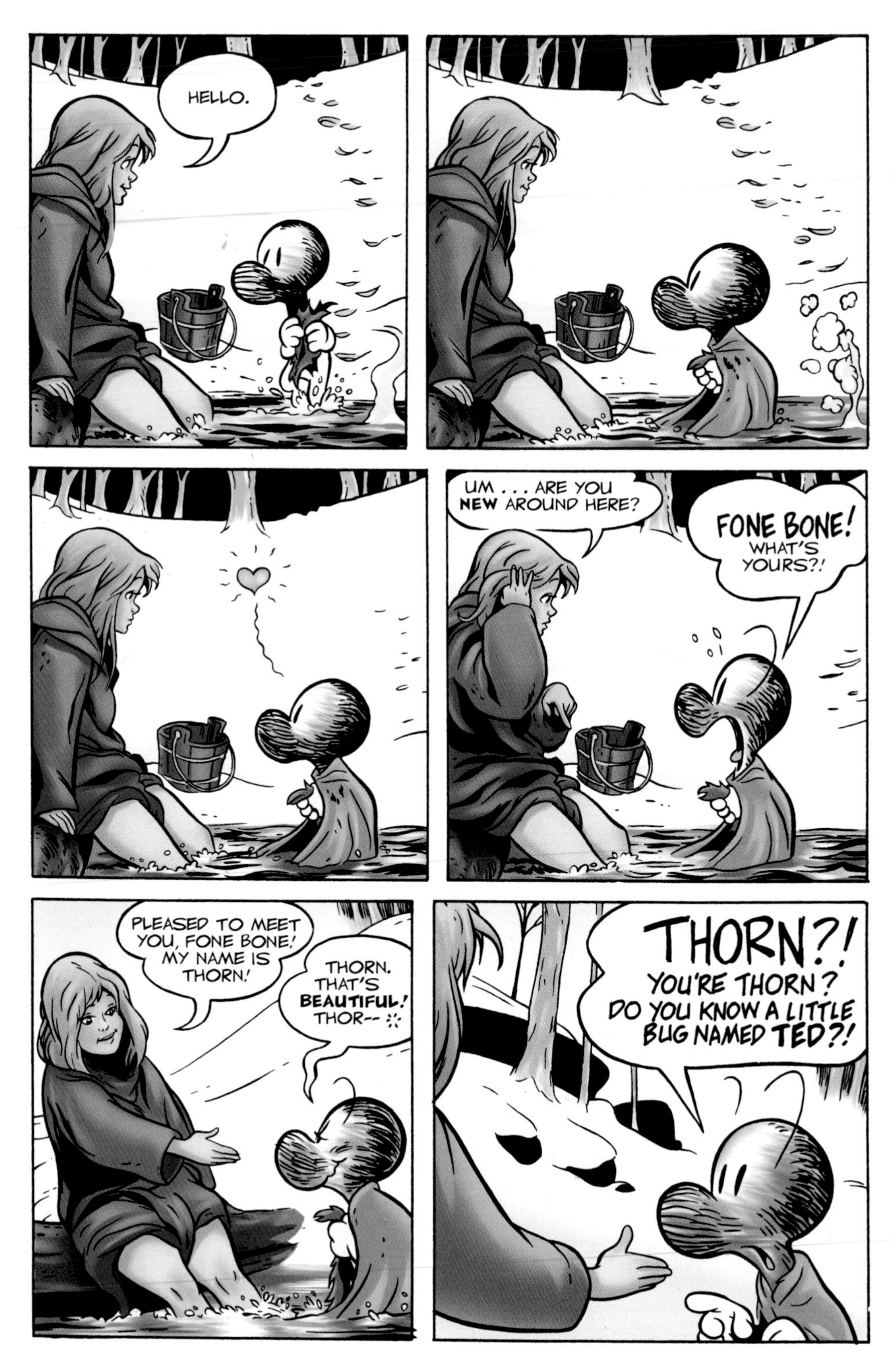
HELLO.
UM . . . ARE YOU NEW AROUND HERE?
FONE BONE! WHAT'S YOURS?!
PLEASED TO MEET YOU, FONE BONE! MY NAME IS THORN!
THORN. THAT'S BEAUTIFUL! THOR--
THORN?! YOU'RE THORN? DO YOU KNOW A LITTLE BUG NAMED TED?!

WHY, YES! I KNOW TED! HE'S A VERY GOOD FRIEND OF MINE!
HOTCHA! THIS IS GREAT!
I'VE BEEN LOOKIN' FOR YOU ALL WINTER!!
YOU HAVE? WHY?
TED! HE TOLD ME TO FIND YOU! HE SAID THAT YOU KNOW EVERYTHING!
WELL, THAT CERTAINLY SOUNDS LIKE TED.
GREAT! THEN YOU CAN HELP ME AND MY COUSINS GET BACK TO BONEVILLE?
COUSINS? YOU MEAN THERE'S MORE OF YOU?
YEAH! THEY'RE STUCK IN THIS VALLEY, TOO! BUT I HAVEN'T SEEN EITHER ONE OF 'EM SINCE WE GOT HIT BY THAT SWARM OF LOCUSTS!
YOU DON'T SAY.
Y'KNOW. . . I SHOULD'VE ASKED THAT DRAGON IF HE'D SEEN MY COUSINS!

YOU SHOULD'VE ASKED WHO?
THE DRAGON! OH . . . WAIT A MINUTE! I GET IT! YOU DON'T BELIEVE IN DRAGONS, DO YOU?
NO. SHOULD I?
NEVER MIND! I DON'T CARE!
ONCE I'M BACK IN BONEVILLE, I'LL NEVER EVEN HAVE TO THINK ABOUT DRAGONS OR THIS CRAZY VALLEY AGAIN!
WELL, I'D LIKE TO HELP. . .
WELL, C'MON! THERE'S NO TIME TO LOSE!!
. . .BUT. . . I'VE NEVER HEARD OF BONEVILLE.
THERE IS A LITTLE VILLAGE DOWN THE ROAD CALLED BARRELHAVEN . . . DOES THAT HELP?
. . .WHAT'S WRONG?
NOTHIN'

FONE BONE?
OH . . . I DON'T BELONG IN THIS FOREST. MY HOME'S ON THE OTHER SIDE OF THE MOUNTAINS . . .
I'M SURE WE CAN GET YOU THROUGH THE MOUNTAINS AS SOON AS THE SNOW MELTS!
IT'S NOT JUST THAT! EVEN IF I COULD GET THROUGH THE MOUNTAINS, I'D NEVER FIND MY WAY BACK ACROSS THE DESERT. YOU WERE MY LAST HOPE.
WELL, LET'S JUST CONCENTRATE ON FINDING YOUR COUSINS. YOU'RE SURE THEY'RE HERE IN THE VALLEY?
PRETTY SURE, UNLESS THE RAT CREATURES GOT 'EM.
DID YOU SAY RAT CREATURES?
LET ME GUESS . . . YOU DON'T BELIEVE IN RAT CREATURES.
OH, YES I DO! HAVE YOU SEEN ONE RECENTLY?
I SAW TWO OF 'EM! TH' DRAGON CHASED 'EM OFF!
NOW LISTEN TO ME . . . THIS IS IMPORTANT! YOU'RE NOT FOOLING AROUND? YOU REALLY SAW TWO RAT CREATURES?
YEAH! I REALLY SAW A DRAGON, TOO! LOOK AT MY HEAD! WHAT DO YOU THINK THIS IS? A TAN?!

HMM. WASH THAT SOOT OFF YOUR FACE. I THINK WE BETTER GET OUT OF HERE!
OKAY WITH ME! WHERE WE GOING?
I LIVE WITH MY GRANDMOTHER JUST THROUGH THE WOODS. WE'LL GO THERE.
WHAT ABOUT YOUR BUCKET? WANT ME TO FILL IT?
OKAY, BUT HURRY!
WHAT'S TH' BIG RUSH ALL OF A SUDDEN? THEY'RE NOT THAT SCARY! IN FACT, THEY'RE KINDA DUMB!
MY! AREN'T YOU BRAVE! I FEEL SAFER ALREADY! C'MON! GIVE ME YOUR HAND!
WELL, I DON'T WANNA BRAG BUT I - - - -
ZING!

WELL, DON'T JUST STAND THERE! LET'S GO!
OH, LISTEN! THE FIRST BIRDS OF SPRING! WE'LL HAVE YOU AND YOUR COUSINS BACK IN BONEVILLE BEFORE YOU KNOW IT!
.....BONEVILLE....?
...WHAT'S BONEVILLE?

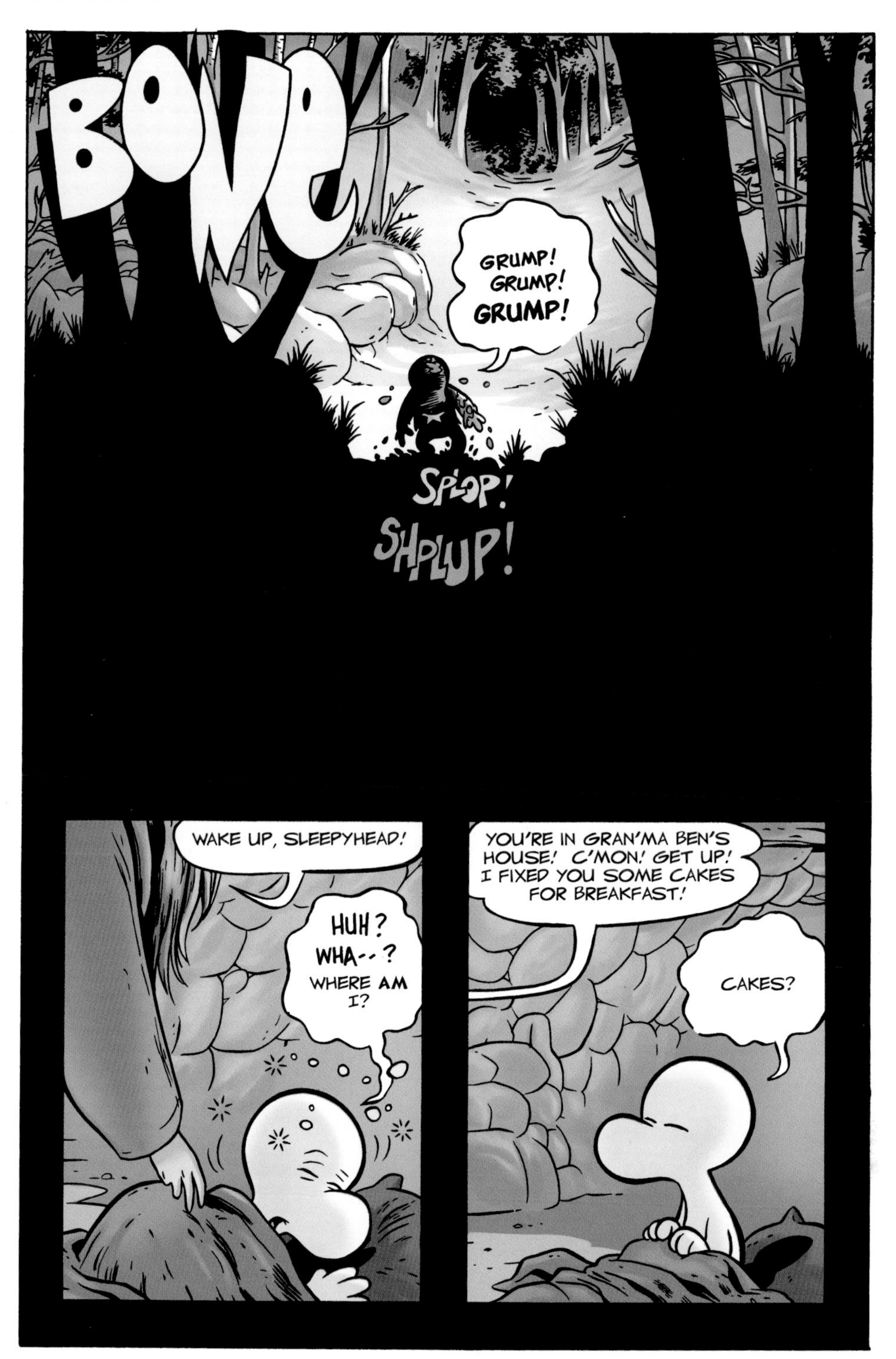
BONE
GRUMP! GRUMP! GRUMP!
SPLOP!
SHPLUP!
WAKE UP, SLEEPYHEAD!
HUH? WHA--? WHERE AM I?
YOU'RE IN GRAN'MA BEN'S HOUSE! C'MON! GET UP! I FIXED YOU SOME CAKES FOR BREAKFAST!
CAKES?

MY! YOU MUST'VE ENJOYED YOUR FIRST NIGHT IN A HOUSE AFTER SLEEPING IN THE WOODS! YOU DIDN'T EVEN HEAR ME WHEN I CAME DOWNSTAIRS!
CAKES?
HERE'S YOUR CAKES! AND HERE'S SOME TEA!
THENK YOU.
HELLO? ARE YOU AWAKE YET, FONE BONE? IT'S ME, THORN!
THORN?

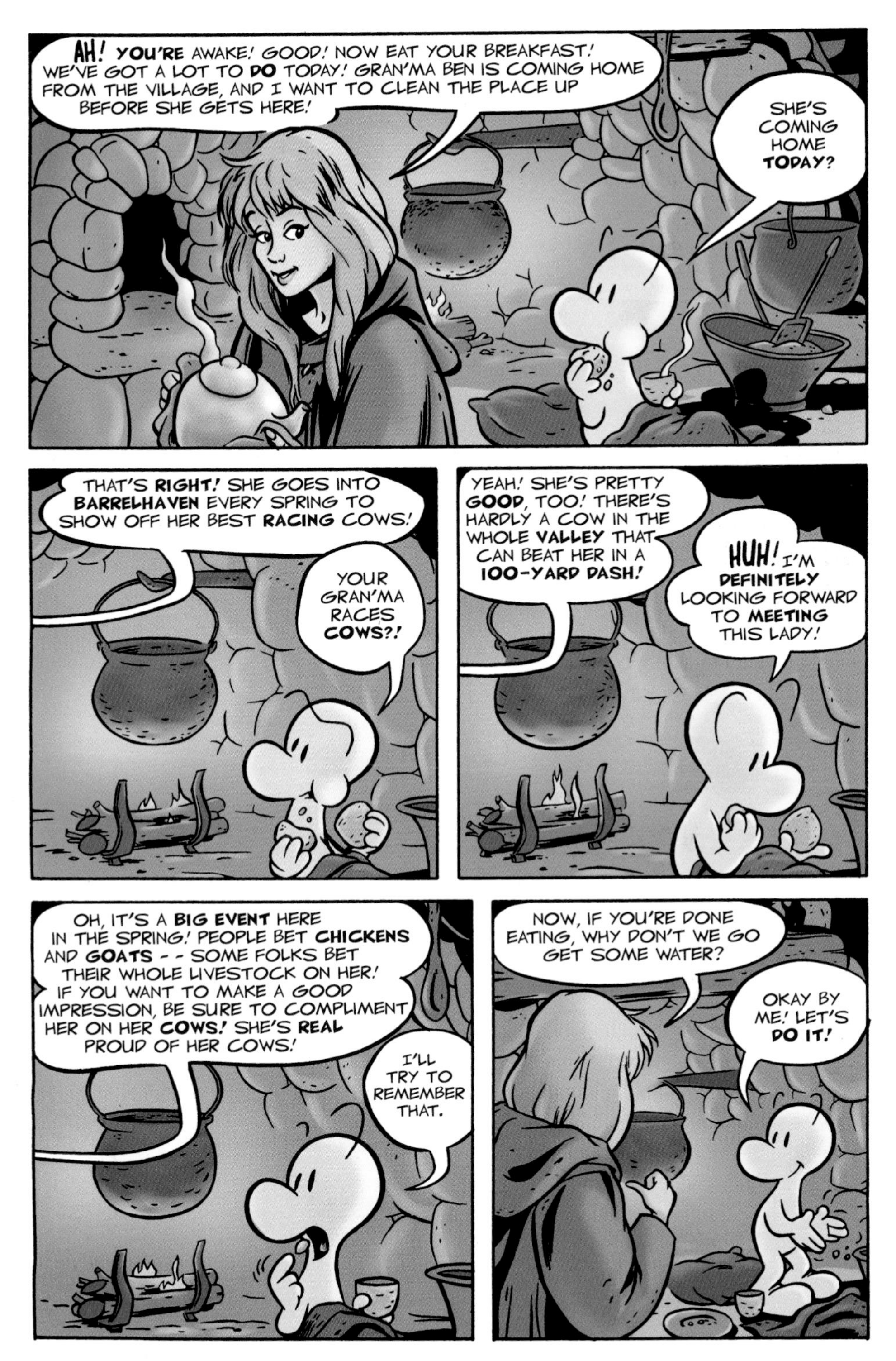
AH! YOU'RE AWAKE! GOOD! NOW EAT YOUR BREAKFAST! WE'VE GOT A LOT TO DO TODAY! GRAN'MA BEN IS COMING HOME FROM THE VILLAGE, AND I WANT TO CLEAN THE PLACE UP BEFORE SHE GETS HERE!
SHE'S COMING HOME TODAY?
THAT'S RIGHT! SHE GOES INTO BARRELHAVEN EVERY SPRING TO SHOW OFF HER BEST RACING COWS!
YOUR GRAN'MA RACES COWS?!
YEAH! SHE'S PRETTY GOOD, TOO! THERE'S HARDLY A COW IN THE WHOLE VALLEY THAT CAN BEAT HER IN A 100-YARD DASH!
HUH! I'M DEFINITELY LOOKING FORWARD TO MEETING THIS LADY!
OH, IT'S A BIG EVENT HERE IN THE SPRING! PEOPLE BET CHICKENS AND GOATS - - SOME FOLKS BET THEIR WHOLE LIVESTOCK ON HER! IF YOU WANT TO MAKE A GOOD IMPRESSION, BE SURE TO COMPLIMENT HER ON HER COWS! SHE'S REAL PROUD OF HER COWS!
I'LL TRY TO REMEMBER THAT.
NOW, IF YOU'RE DONE EATING, WHY DON'T WE GO GET SOME WATER?
OKAY BY ME! LET'S DO IT!

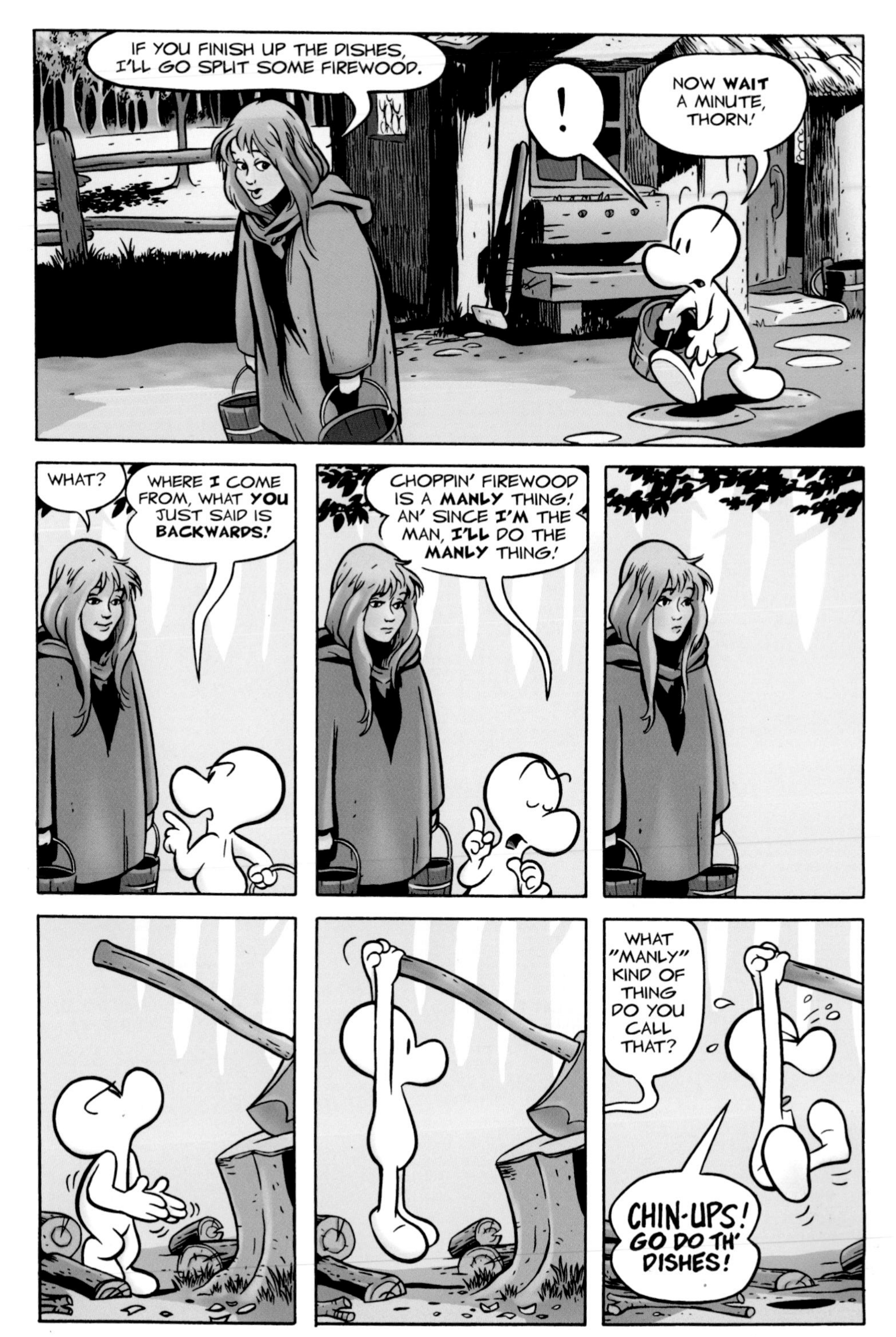
IF YOU FINISH UP THE DISHES, I'LL GO SPLIT SOME FIREWOOD.
!
NOW WAIT A MINUTE, THORN!
WHAT?
WHERE I COME FROM, WHAT YOU JUST SAID IS BACKWARDS!
CHOPPIN' FIREWOOD IS A MANLY THING! AN' SINCE I'M THE MAN, I'LL DO THE MANLY THING!
WHAT "MANLY" KIND OF THING DO YOU CALL THAT?
CHIN-UPS! GO DO TH' DISHES!

HOW ABOUT IF WE GET THE FIREWOOD LATER?
SIGH.
SO . . . DO YOU THINK YOUR GRAN'MA WILL MIND ME STAYIN' WITH YOU GUYS? I MEAN-- I DON'T WANNA CAUSE ANY PROBLEMS!
SHE WON'T MIND! SHE WOULDN'T MAKE YOU GO BACK OUT IN THE WOODS -- ESPECIALLY WITH THOSE RAT CREATURES AROUND!
I HOPE NOT.
JUST DO ME ONE FAVOR! WHEN GRAN'MA BEN GETS HERE, TRY NOT TO MENTION YOUR FRIEND THE DRAGON!
WHY NOT?
BECAUSE DRAGONS DON'T EXIST, THAT'S WHY!
WHAT DO YOU MEAN? YOU BELIEVE IN RAT CREATURES! WHY DON'T YOU BELIEVE IN DRAGONS?
BECAUSE EVERYBODY BELIEVES IN RAT CREATURES! BUT YOU'RE THE ONLY ONE WHO'S EVER SEEN A DRAGON!
I DON'T BELIEVE IT!

DO YOU HAVE DRAGONS BACK IN BONEVILLE?
OF COURSE NOT!
WELL?
WELL, WE DON'T HAVE BIGMOUTHED, DROOLING, RAT-LIKE MONSTERS, EITHER! UNLESS YOU COUNT MY COUSIN PHONEY BONE!
AN' YOU KNOW WHAT ELSE? I THINK THAT DRAGON IS FOLLOWIN' ME AROUND!
FONE BONE! WE'VE BEEN OVER THIS A HUNDRED TIMES!
BUT I'M TELLIN' YA, I SAW ONE! HE HAD A GOATEE, 'N' A CIGARETTE, 'N' BIG OL' HAIRY EARS LIKE THIS!
DRAGONS ARE MAKE-BELIEVE! YOU WERE SEEING THINGS!
THANKS FOR THE SUPPORT, THORN! YOU KNOW, THAT'S WHAT THE DRAGON WANTS YOU TO THINK! HE DOESN'T WANT YOU TO KNOW HE EXISTS!
ACTUALLY, I JUST WANT HER TO THINK YOU'RE NUTS!
OH, SHUT UP!

HEY!
COME BACK HERE WITH MY BUCKET, YOU!
FONE BONE? WHAT ARE YOU DOING?
I'M COMIN'! I'M COMIN'!
HERE... WHAT DO YOU WANT ME TO DO WITH THIS?
OH! THAT'S MY KNAPSACK! I RAN BACK TO MY PLACE LAST NIGHT TO GET MY BOOKS!
YOU HAVE BOOKS IN HERE?
YEAH. WHEN ME AN' MY COUSINS GOT RUN OUT OF BONEVILLE, I PACKED SOME STUFF FOR US TO READ...
I LOVE BOOKS! OOH! WHAT ARE THESE?!
JUST SOME COMIC BOOKS. I BROUGHT THOSE FOR SMILEY BONE.
I'VE NEVER SEEN ONE BEFORE!

YOU HAVEN'T? YOU MUST'VE HAD A DEPRIVED CHILDHOOD. THESE I BROUGHT FOR PHONEY BONE . . . THEY'RE FINANCIAL MAGAZINES!
DIDN'T YOU BRING ANYTHING FOR YOURSELF?
SURE! THIS IS MOBY DICK! IT'S MY FAVORITE BOOK! I'VE READ IT THREE TIMES!
WHAT'S IT ABOUT?
UH . . . ARE YOU SURE YOU WANT TO KNOW? EVERY TIME I TRY TO TELL PEOPLE ABOUT MOBY DICK THEIR EYES GLAZE OVER!
TRY ME.
OKAY! IT'S ABOUT A WHALING VOYAGE, AN' THIS GUY ISHMAEL ----
Z
HA. HA. VERY FUNNY.
WHAT ELSE HAVE YOU GOT IN HERE?
LET'S SEE . . . A BLANKET . . . AN OLD MAP THAT SMILEY FOUND . . . . . .

THAT'S ABOUT IT! THE ONE THING I DIDN'T BRING ENOUGH OF WAS FOOD AND WATER! WELL, TH' TWO THINGS ....
WHY ARE YOU MAKING THAT FACE?
I DON'T KNOW .... SOMETHING ABOUT THIS MAP IS FAMILIAR ...
REALLY? SMILEY FOUND IT OUT IN TH' DESERT RIGHT BEFORE WE GOT SPLIT UP.
IT REMINDS ME OF A DREAM I USED TO HAVE ...
WHOA. AND YOU THINK MY STORIES ARE STRANGE!
ARE YOU OKAY?
I'M FINE, LET'S JUST FORGET IT. C'MON, GRAN'MA WILL BE HERE SOON ...

GRUMP!
GRUMP!
GRUMP!

GRUMP!
SPLOP
SPLOOOSH

OOOH! WAIT'LL I GET MY HANDS ON THAT COUSIN OF MINE!

I CAN'T BELIEVE FONE BONE WOULD JUST LEAVE ME OUT HERE WANDERING AROUND HELPLESS AND HUNGRY!

I'LL BET HE'S BACK IN BONEVILLE RIGHT NOW. SITTING IN MY HOUSE, EATING MY FOOD!
GLORP!
RUMBLE!
GRRRR

GROWL!
HEY! SHUT UP! I JUST ATE A STICK AN HOUR AGO! WHAT DO YOU WANT FROM ME?!

SLURK
GUKK
BURRRRP!
SIGH.
WHAT A TRAVESTY! TH' MOST CHERISHED AND RESPECTED (NOT TO MENTION WEALTHIEST!) BONE IN BONEVILLE-- OUT IN TH' WOODS-- FENDING OFF TH' ELEMENTS WITH HIS BARE HANDS!
FORCED TO EKE OUT A MISERABLE EXISTENCE AMIDST TH' ROCKS 'N' MUD!!
OH, CRUEL, CRUEL, FATE! WHY HAVE YOU ABANDONED YOUR MOST BELOVED SON?!
GOD, I PITY ME.
HEY, YOU! WAKE UP!
MM?

THE NAME'S PHONEY BONE... TH' RICHEST BONE IN BONEVILLE! YOU'VE PROBABLY HEARD OF ME! I'M LOOKIN' FOR A GUY NAMED FONE BONE. YOU SEEN HIM?
HEY! LET'S KICK THAT PEA-SIZED DINOSAUR BRAIN INTO HIGH GEAR, HUH?
WOULD IT HELP IF I ASKED TH' QUESTION AGAIN SLOWER?
HAVE......YOU.....
...SEEN FONE BONE..... ....A-ROUND?
UH, HEY, THERE, MISTER! MAYBE YOU BETTER LET ME HELP YOU!
MAYBE I BETTER! IT COULD BE DAYS BEFORE TH' MESSAGE REACHES THIS GUY'S BRAIN!

HOW 'BOUT WE TAKE A FEW STEPS OFF TO STARBOARD... OUTTA FIRIN' RANGE ... AN' I'LL ANSWER YER QUESTIONS FOR YA.
OH, YEAH? AN' WHO ARE YOU?
I'M TED! I'M A BUG!
SPARE ME TH' DETAILS, FRIEND! I'M LOOKIN' FOR A GUY NAMED FONE BONE. YOU SEEN HIM?
BONE? OH, YEAH! I SEEN HIM!
YOU HAVE?! I'M SAVED! WHERE IS HE?
DON'T KNOW. AIN'T SEEN HIM SINCE BEFORE SHE SNOWED.
HA! A LIKELY STORY! BUG! TAKE ME TO YOUR LEADER!
TAKE YOU TO MY LEADER?
C'MON! C'MON! I AIN'T GOT ALL DAY!
WHO SHOULD I TAKES YA TO?
I NEED ANSWERS, BUG! I DEMAND SATISFACTION!
I GUESS I COULD TAKE YA TO SEE THORN'S GRAN'MA ...
FINE. FINE. WHAT-EVER!
BUT I GOTS TA WARN YA ... SHE'S A OL' LADY, AN' SHE MIGHT NOT TAKE TO YER ATTITUDE MUCH ...
DON'T WORRY ABOUT ME, BUG! THERE AIN'T A WOMAN ALIVE WHO CAN RESIST MY CHARMS!

OKEE DOKEE... I WAS JES WARNIN' YA, THAT'S ALL.
WELL, MOVE IT OUT, BUG! THIS IS TAKING FOREVER ON THOSE LITTLE LEGS OF YOURS!
OKEE DOKEE...
HI, GRAN'MA! HOW YOU DOIN'?
WELL, HELLO, TED, DEAR!
GRAN'MA, THIS HERE FELLA BEEN ASKIN' TA MEET YA!
OH, HE LOOKS LIKE SUCH A NICE YOUNG MAN. WOULD HE LIKE TO RIDE ONE OF MY RACING COWS?
NO, I DON'T WANNA RIDE ONE OF YER STUPID COWS!
TED, DEAR, I THINK YOU'D BETTER LEAVE. I'M GONNA TEAR THIS LITTLE FELLA APART FROM THE INSIDE OUT.
YES, MA'M. (SEE YA AROUND, PAL.)

DO YOU LIKE APPLE PIE, FONE BONE?
LIKE IT? IT'S MY FAVORITE HOBBY!
WELL, DON'T GET TOO EXCITED!

THIS IS FOR GRAN'MA -- SHE LOVES MY SPECIAL APPLE PIE...

...AND WE WANT TO BE REAL NICE TO GRAN'MA BEFORE WE ASK ABOUT YOU STAYING HERE!
CLINK
CLINK

HEY! WHAT'S GOIN' ON?! TH' WHOLE CABIN'S STARTIN' TO SHAKE!
IT'S GRAN'MA! SHE'S HOME!
YOUR GRAN'MA?! IT SOUNDS LIKE A STAMPEDE!
THAT'S HER! SHE MUST BE RACING ONE OF THE COWS!
LOOK OUTSIDE! THAT'S HER FASTEST COW COMING ACROSS THE CLEARING!
NO WAY!
AND HERE COMES GRAN'MA! C'MON, GRAN'MA!
SHE'S GONNA OUTRUN THAT COW?! SHE'LL HAVE A HEART ATTACK!
HEY! DO YOU SEE THAT? THERE'S SOMETHING ON THE COW.
WHAT? WHERE?
--THERE'S SOMEONE RIDING THE COW!
OH, MY GOD! IT'S PHONEY BONE!

WHAT'S HE DOING?
IT LOOKS LIKE HE'S HEADING STRAIGHT FOR US!
HE'S OUT OF CONTROL!
HOLY COW! LET'S GET OUTTA HERE!!
SCREEECH!
MOO!
ZZZEEE
KABONG!
CRASH!
WHAT HAPPENED?!
JEEZ! YOUR GRAN'MA STOPPED TH' COW BY TH' TAIL!
MOO!

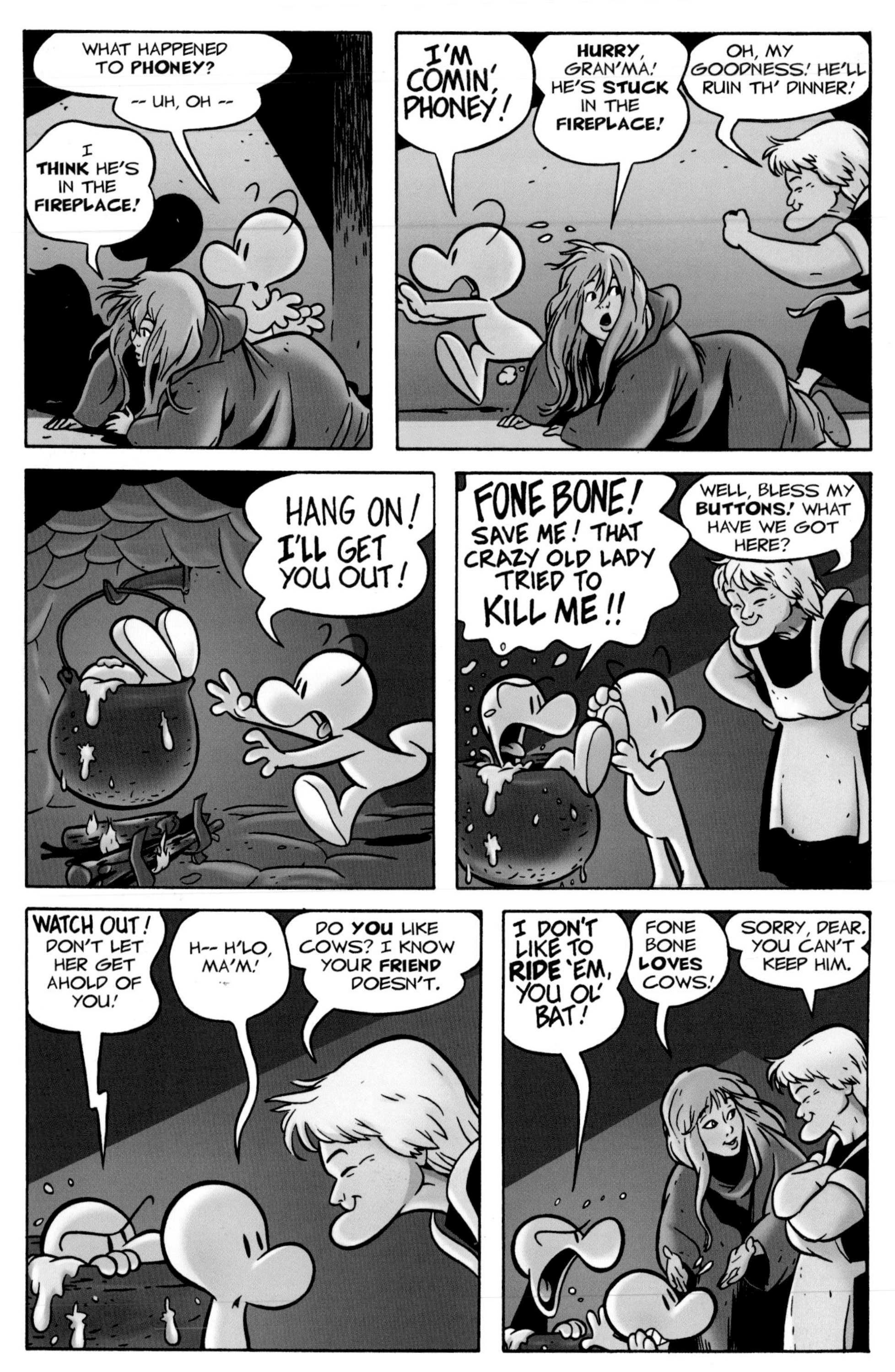
WHAT HAPPENED TO PHONEY?
-- UH, OH --
I THINK HE'S IN THE FIREPLACE!
I'M COMIN', PHONEY!
HURRY, GRAN'MA! HE'S STUCK IN THE FIREPLACE!
OH, MY GOODNESS! HE'LL RUIN TH' DINNER!
HANG ON! I'LL GET YOU OUT!
FONE BONE! SAVE ME! THAT CRAZY OLD LADY TRIED TO KILL ME!!
WELL, BLESS MY BUTTONS! WHAT HAVE WE GOT HERE?
WATCH OUT! DON'T LET HER GET AHOLD OF YOU!
H-- H'LO, MA'M!
DO YOU LIKE COWS? I KNOW YOUR FRIEND DOESN'T.
I DON'T LIKE TO RIDE 'EM, YOU OL' BAT!
FONE BONE LOVES COWS!
SORRY, DEAR. YOU CAN'T KEEP HIM.

BUT--
NO BUTS. I DON'T WANT ANY PETS RUNNING AROUND TH' HOUSE.
GRAN'MA! THEY'RE NOT PETS!
CAN YOU MILK 'EM? IF YOU CAN'T MILK 'EM, THEY'RE PETS!
THAT'S IT! I'M OUTTA HERE!
GRAN'MA!
SAY... IS THAT APPLE PIE I SMELL?
YES! I BAKED ONE OF MY SPECIAL PIES JUST FOR YOU!
WHAT A SWEET THING YOU ARE!
QUICK!
WHILE SHE'S DISTRACTED!
HOLD IT! THORN THINKS GRAN'MA BEN CAN HELP US GET BACK TO BONEVILLE!
IT'S NOT WORTH IT! LET GO OF ME!
WOULD YOU WAIT A MINUTE?!! WE CAN EXPLAIN EVERYTHING!
HELP! HELP! THEY'VE DESTROYED MY COUSIN'S BRAIN!!
OH, MY GOD! THEY'VE ALREADY MILKED YOU, HAVEN'T THEY?!!

GRAN'MA, THEY'RE BONES! THEY COME FROM A PLACE CALLED BONEVILLE! AND THEY NEED OUR HELP TO GET BACK!
WHERE'S SMILEY?
SMILEY? I THOUGHT HE WAS WITH YOU!
YOU HAVEN'T SEEN HIM SINCE WE SPLIT UP? BUT I KNOW HE'S IN TH' VALLEY! I FOUND ONE OF HIS CIGAR BUTTS!
TH' LAST TIME I SAW THAT CHOWDERHEAD, HE WAS SAYIN' HOW COOL IT WAS THAT WE WERE ABOUT TO BE PULVERIZED BY INSECTS!
YEAH! THAT'S TH' LAST TIME I SAW HIM, TOO...
AW, QUIT YER WORRYIN'! WHY DON'T YA INTRODUCE ME TO YER GOOD-LOOKIN' FRIEND, HERE?
OH! UH... PHONEY, THIS IS THORN! THORN, PHONEY.
SO, WHAT'VE YOU BEEN DOIN' WITH MY COUSIN? YOU TWO GOT A LITTLE THING GOIN', OR WHAT?
PHONEY!
NO, HUH? FIGURES! WHAT'D YA DO? BORE HER TO DEATH TALKIN' ABOUT MOBY DICK?

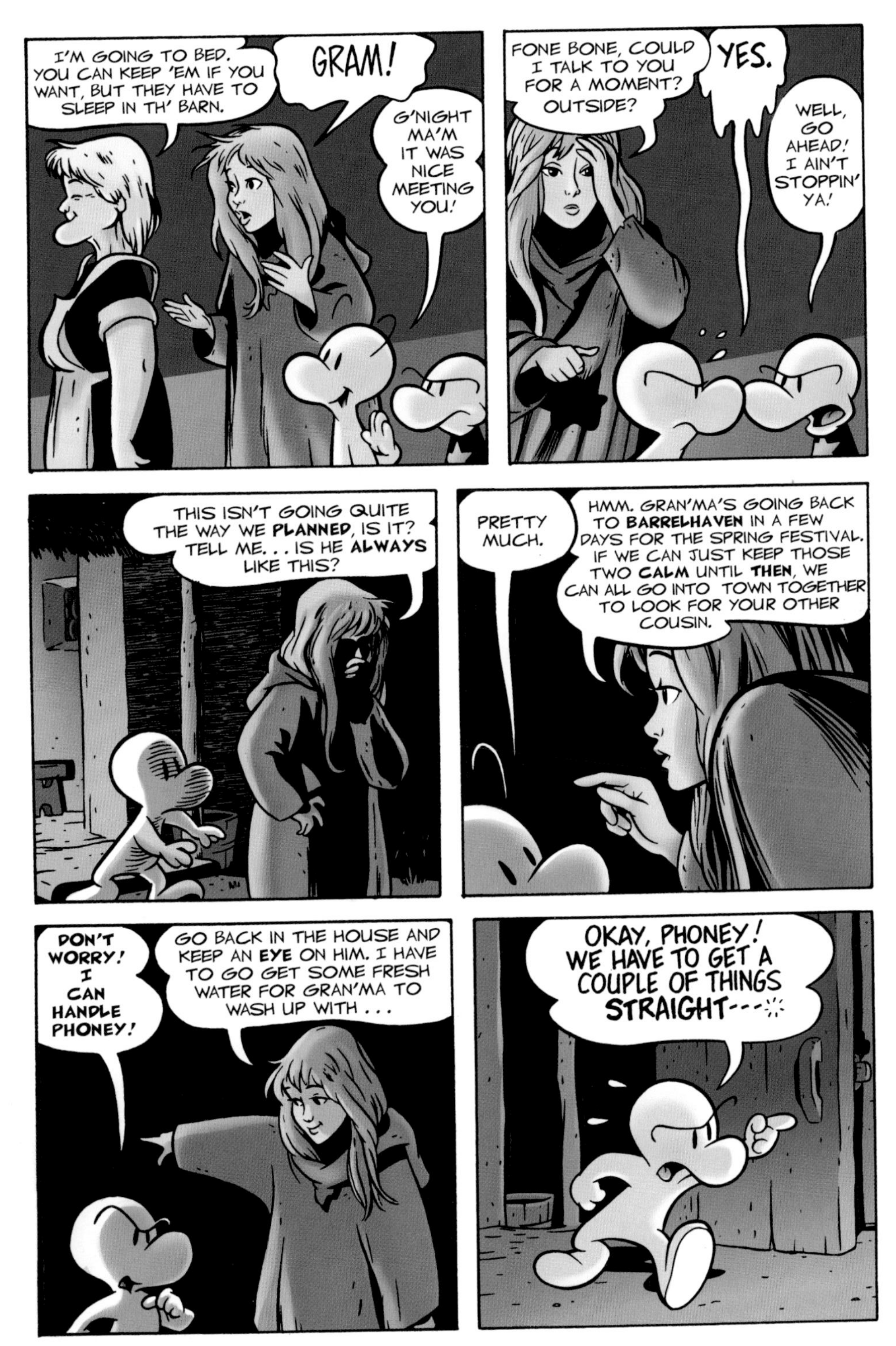
I'M GOING TO BED. YOU CAN KEEP 'EM IF YOU WANT, BUT THEY HAVE TO SLEEP IN TH' BARN.
GRAM!
G'NIGHT MA'M IT WAS NICE MEETING YOU!
FONE BONE, COULD I TALK TO YOU FOR A MOMENT? OUTSIDE?
YES.
WELL, GO AHEAD! I AIN'T STOPPIN' YA!
THIS ISN'T GOING QUITE THE WAY WE PLANNED, IS IT? TELL ME... IS HE ALWAYS LIKE THIS?
PRETTY MUCH.
HMM. GRAN'MA'S GOING BACK TO BARRELHAVEN IN A FEW DAYS FOR THE SPRING FESTIVAL. IF WE CAN JUST KEEP THOSE TWO CALM UNTIL THEN, WE CAN ALL GO INTO TOWN TOGETHER TO LOOK FOR YOUR OTHER COUSIN.
GO BACK IN THE HOUSE AND KEEP AN EYE ON HIM. I HAVE TO GO GET SOME FRESH WATER FOR GRAN'MA TO WASH UP WITH . . .
DON'T WORRY! I CAN HANDLE PHONEY!
OKAY, PHONEY! WE HAVE TO GET A COUPLE OF THINGS STRAIGHT---

WHAT ARE YOU DOING ?!! ... THAT PIE WAS FOR GRAN'MA BEN! THORN WILL KILL US WHEN SHE FINDS OUT YOU TOOK IT!
WHAT'S TH' MATTER? YOU AFRAID OF GETTIN' CAUGHT? QUIT BEIN' A CHICKEN!
FONE BONE!! PHONEY BONE!! YOU BETTER NOT BE EATING THAT PIE!
HONK!
WELL, BOYS... I CAN SEE WE'RE OFF TO A GOOD START!
WE HAVEN'T SEEN IT! HONEST!
ERP!

BONE
PHONEY!
THAT'S TH' SECOND TIME IN TWO DAYS THAT YOU'VE SPILLED TH' MILK!
I CAN'T HELP IT. IT'S A DISGUSTING WAY TO GET MILK!
IT'S HOW YOU GET MILK! THERE'S NOTHING DISGUSTING ABOUT IT!
IT'S DISGUSTING THAT I HAVE TO DO IT! I QUIT!

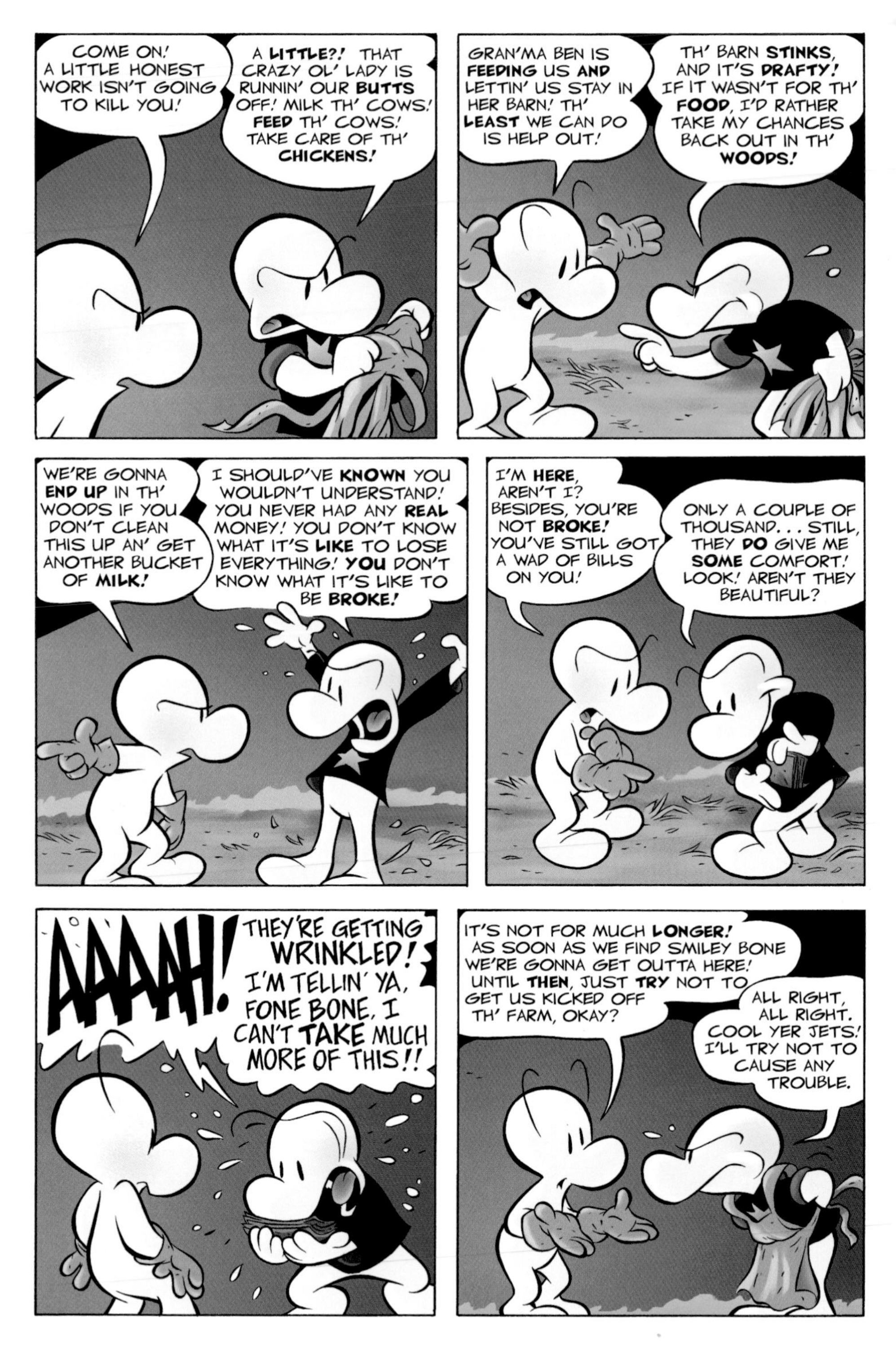
COME ON! A LITTLE HONEST WORK ISN'T GOING TO KILL YOU!
A LITTLE?! THAT CRAZY OL' LADY IS RUNNIN' OUR BUTTS OFF! MILK TH' COWS! FEED TH' COWS! TAKE CARE OF TH' CHICKENS!
GRAN'MA BEN IS FEEDING US AND LETTIN' US STAY IN HER BARN! TH' LEAST WE CAN DO IS HELP OUT!
TH' BARN STINKS, AND IT'S DRAFTY! IF IT WASN'T FOR TH' FOOD, I'D RATHER TAKE MY CHANCES BACK OUT IN TH' WOODS!
WE'RE GONNA END UP IN TH' WOODS IF YOU DON'T CLEAN THIS UP AN' GET ANOTHER BUCKET OF MILK!
I SHOULD'VE KNOWN YOU WOULDN'T UNDERSTAND! YOU NEVER HAD ANY REAL MONEY! YOU DON'T KNOW WHAT IT'S LIKE TO LOSE EVERYTHING! YOU DON'T KNOW WHAT IT'S LIKE TO BE BROKE!
I'M HERE, AREN'T I? BESIDES, YOU'RE NOT BROKE! YOU'VE STILL GOT A WAD OF BILLS ON YOU!
ONLY A COUPLE OF THOUSAND. . . STILL, THEY DO GIVE ME SOME COMFORT! LOOK! AREN'T THEY BEAUTIFUL?
AAAAH!
THEY'RE GETTING WRINKLED! I'M TELLIN' YA, FONE BONE, I CAN'T TAKE MUCH MORE OF THIS!!
IT'S NOT FOR MUCH LONGER! AS SOON AS WE FIND SMILEY BONE WE'RE GONNA GET OUTTA HERE! UNTIL THEN, JUST TRY NOT TO GET US KICKED OFF TH' FARM, OKAY?
ALL RIGHT, ALL RIGHT. COOL YER JETS! I'LL TRY NOT TO CAUSE ANY TROUBLE.

GOOD! I'VE GOTTA GO FIND THORN . . . I PROMISED I'D HELP HER CHURN BUTTER TODAY!
YEAH, YEAH. STICK SOME HAY IN MY TEETH AN' CALL ME GOOBER!
CHEER UP, PHONEY! BREAKFAST WILL BE READY SOON!
RRRRR.
MORNIN', BONE!
GOOD MORNIN', GRAN'MA! YOU ALL SET FOR OUR BIG TRIP TO BARRELHAVEN TOMORROW?
I'M STILL PACKIN'- - I SEEM TO BE MISSING A PAIR OF BLOOMERS, THOUGH . . . YOU AN' YOUR COUSIN WOULDN'T KNOW ANYTHING ABOUT THAT, WOULD YOU?
NO, MA'M!
HMMF. HOW ARE THINGS GOIN' IN TH' BARN THIS MORNIN'? ANY MORE TROUBLE?
UH... NO. PHONEY'S JUST GETTING TH' MILK NOW, I THINK!

THAT'S GOOD. WE'VE GOT A TIGHT SCHEDULE----
YES, MA'M! THORN AND I ARE GOING TO CHURN BUTTER, AND BAKE THESE LITTLE BREAD THINGS WITH STUFF IN 'EM TO TAKE ON TH' JOURNEY-
OH, NO . . . .
WHAT? DON'T YOU WANT TH' BREAD THINGS?
IT'S NOT TH' **BREAD**, BONE! IT'S TH' **GITCHY FEELIN'!** --IT JUST COME **AT** ME OUTTA TH' **BLUE!**
TH' **GITCHY FEELIN'**? WHAT'S THAT?
TH' **GITCHY!** IT'S A **TERRIBLE** FEELIN' THAT MAKES YOUR HEAD **SWIM**, AN' YOUR LEGS **WOBBLE!** IT'S A POWERFUL **OMEN** OF **BAD THINGS** TO **COME!**
. . .THERE . . . IT'S STARTIN' TO PASS. MAYBE WHATEVER'S GOIN' TO HAPPEN WON'T BE SO BAD. . .
ARE YOU OKAY?
IT'S GONE NOW. BUT TH' GITCHY FEELIN' IS **NEVER** WRONG! YOU KEEP AN EYE ON THAT COUSIN OF YOURS, YOU HEAR?
YES MA'M!

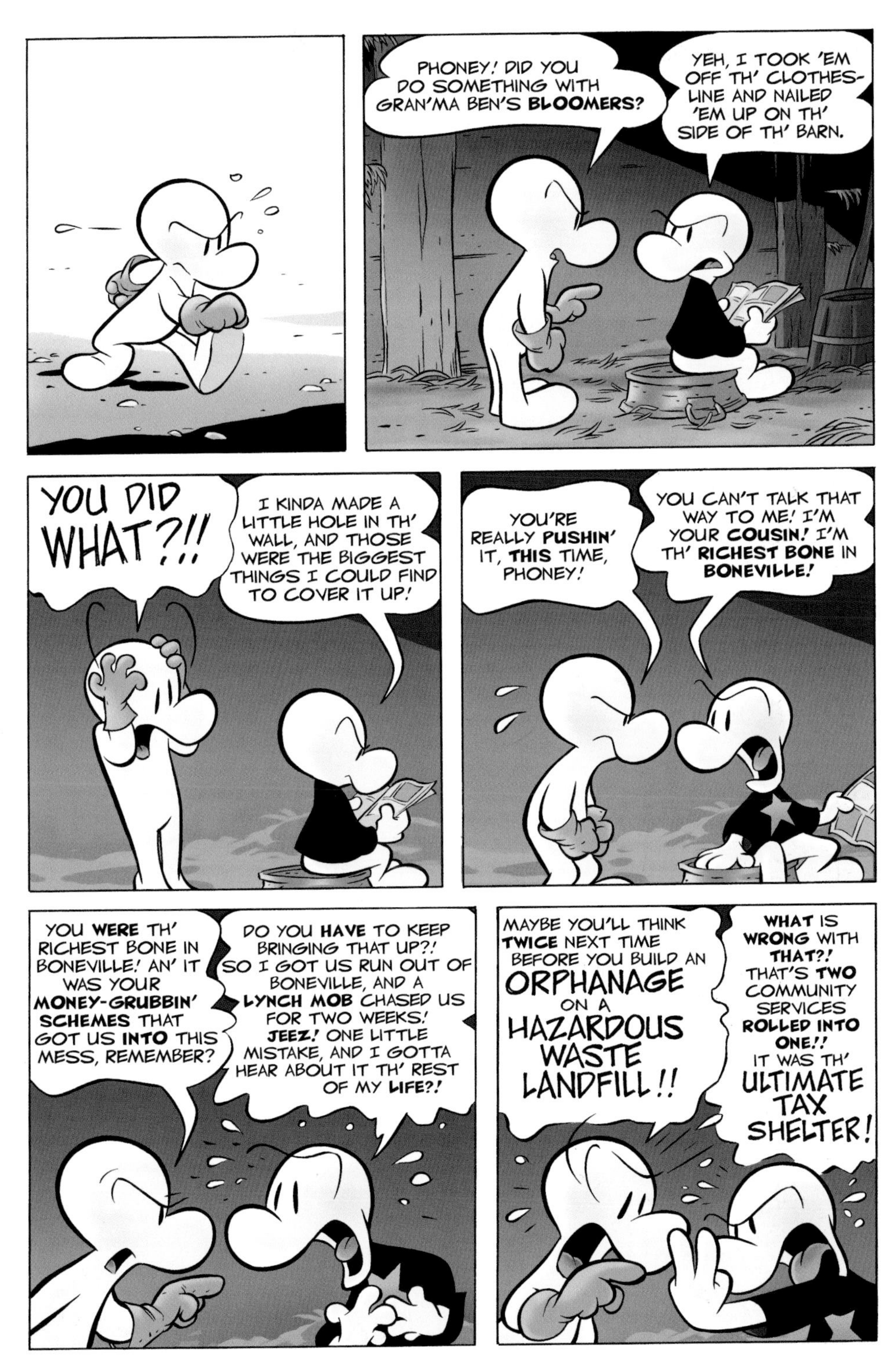
PHONEY! DID YOU DO SOMETHING WITH GRAN'MA BEN'S BLOOMERS?
YEH, I TOOK 'EM OFF TH' CLOTHES-LINE AND NAILED 'EM UP ON TH' SIDE OF TH' BARN.
YOU DID WHAT?!!
I KINDA MADE A LITTLE HOLE IN TH' WALL, AND THOSE WERE THE BIGGEST THINGS I COULD FIND TO COVER IT UP!
YOU'RE REALLY PUSHIN' IT, THIS TIME, PHONEY!
YOU CAN'T TALK THAT WAY TO ME! I'M YOUR COUSIN! I'M TH' RICHEST BONE IN BONEVILLE!
YOU WERE TH' RICHEST BONE IN BONEVILLE! AN' IT WAS YOUR MONEY-GRUBBIN' SCHEMES THAT GOT US INTO THIS MESS, REMEMBER?
DO YOU HAVE TO KEEP BRINGING THAT UP?! SO I GOT US RUN OUT OF BONEVILLE, AND A LYNCH MOB CHASED US FOR TWO WEEKS! JEEZ! ONE LITTLE MISTAKE, AND I GOTTA HEAR ABOUT IT TH' REST OF MY LIFE?!
MAYBE YOU'LL THINK TWICE NEXT TIME BEFORE YOU BUILD AN ORPHANAGE ON A HAZARDOUS WASTE LANDFILL!!
WHAT IS WRONG WITH THAT?! THAT'S TWO COMMUNITY SERVICES ROLLED INTO ONE!! IT WAS TH' ULTIMATE TAX SHELTER!

YOU NEVER LEARN, DO YOU?
I SHOULDA STUCK WITH MY FIRST IDEA!
WHAT? COMBINING A SLAUGHTERHOUSE WITH A PETTING ZOO?! OH, YEAH! THAT WAS BRILLIANT!
AHH! WHAT DO YOU KNOW?
CAN'T YOU MAKE IT THROUGH ONE MORE DAY WITHOUT GETTING US IN TROUBLE? WE'RE GOIN' INTO TOWN WITH GRAN'MA TOMORROW!
WHAT ARE WE WAITIN' FOR HER FOR? LET'S BLOW THIS POPSICLE STAND NOW!
TOMORROW IS TH' FIRST DAY OF TH' SPRING FAIR! THIS'LL BE OUR BEST SHOT AT FINDING SMILEY BONE!
GRAN'MA SAID THAT LAST WEEK PEOPLE WERE ALREADY COMIN' IN FROM ALL OVER TH' VALLEY- - - SETTIN' UP BOOTHS AN' GETTIN' READY!
WELL, I FIGURE -- IF SMILEY'S SOMEWHERE IN TH' VALLEY, HE'S BOUND TO HAVE HEARD ABOUT GRAN'MA'S COW RACE! YOU KNOW HOW MUCH HE LIKES TO BET ON RACES!
HO -- BACK UP! YOU MEAN PEOPLE ACTUALLY BET MONEY ON THAT OL' BAG TO BEAT A COW IN A FOOTRACE?
I KNOW! IT'S CRAZY, BUT THORN SAYS IT'S A BIG DEAL HERE! SOME FOLKS BET EVERYTHING THEY'VE GOT!
OKAY, FONE BONE! I'LL BE GOOD! I POSITIVELY GUARANTEE YOU WON'T HEAR ANOTHER PEEP OUTTA ME ALL DAY!

REALLY?
YEAH, NOW GET OFF MY BACK! GO CHURN SOME BUTTER WITH THORN! I'VE GOT STUFF TO DO!
WHAT? WHAT ARE YOU UP TO?
NOTHING! I SAID I WON'T MESS UP YOUR PLAN TO GO INTO TOWN TO LOOK FOR SMILEY, AN' I **MEANT** IT!
AND I WON'T HEAR A **PEEP** OUTTA YOU TH' REST OF TH' **DAY**, RIGHT?
RIGHT! JEEZ! DO YA WANT IT IN **WRITING?!**
DO YOU HAVE A PIECE OF PAPER?
I THINK I HEAR THORN CALLIN' YA.
REALLY?! OKAY, PHONEY! SEE YA TONIGHT!

YEP, YOU WON'T HEAR A PEEP OUTTA ME, 'CAUSE I AIN'T GONNA BE HERE!
FONE BONE WON'T MIND IF I BORROW A FEW OF HIS THINGS . . . I MIGHT NEED 'EM ON MY WAY TO TOWN . . .
SOUNDS LIKE A LOTTA MONEY'S GONNA CHANGE HANDS TOMORROW, AN' I DON'T SEE WHY GRAN'MA BEN SHOULD HOG IT ALL!
NO, SIRREE! IF THERE'S BOOKMAKIN' TO BE DONE, I'M TH' MAN TO DO IT!

HEY, THORN! WHERE WE GOIN'?
DOWN TO THE SPRINGS!
OH, FONE BONE, YOU'RE GOING TO **LOVE** THE FESTIVAL! WE'LL SEE JUGGLERS, AND TUMBLERS, AND SINGERS! AND MY **FAVORITE** PART- - THE **BOOTHS!**
THERE ARE **ROWS** AND **ROWS** OF **BOOTHS**, AND YOU CAN BUY THE MOST **AMAZING** THINGS! THEY HAVE **HONEY**, AND **PEACOCK FEATHERS**, AND **SILK ROBES!**
I USUALLY ONLY GET TO LOOK- - BUT **THIS** YEAR I'M GOING TO GET A BOTTLE OF **DYE** FROM THE SOUTH, AND I'M GOING TO MAKE A BEAUTIFUL **BLUE DRESS!**
HOW COME WE DIDN'T BRING ANY BUCKETS TO CARRY TH' WATER BACK IN?
WE'RE NOT GETTING WATER.
WE'RE TAKING A BATH!
A BATH? WHAT **KIND** OF BATH?
OHMYGOSH
YOU WANT TO GET CLEANED UP FOR THE FESTIVAL, DON'T YOU? C'MON!

WOULD YOU BRING ME THE SOAP? I LEFT IT IN THE POCKET OF MY DRESS . . . .
I'VE NEVER DONE THIS BEFORE . . .
DON'T BE SO NERVOUS! YOU NEVER WEAR CLOTHES ANYWAY!
. . . UM . . . FONE BONE, COULD YOU BE A LITTLE MORE CAREFUL WITH THE SOAP?
UH . . .
WHAT?
THE SOAP, SILLY! YOU JUST ATE THE WHOLE BAR!

RRRR. THERE WAS A PATH HERE A SECOND AGO! WHAT HAPPENED TO IT?
CRUNCH
CRACK
SNAP
WHY DOESN'T SOMEBODY BUILD SOME ROADS IN THIS PLACE?!
HMM. MAYBE I SHOULD LOOK INTO THAT....
I COULD BUILD A TOLL ROAD!
YEAH! I CAN ALMOST HEAR THOSE LITTLE COINS CALLING OUT TO ME NOW--
HELLO, BONE!
OVER HERE! IN TH' TREE!
WHAT ARE YOU KIDS DOIN' HANGIN' AROUND HERE? GET A JOB!
SORRY, MISTER! WE THOUGHT YOU WERE SOMEONE ELSE!
WE THOUGHT YOU WERE FONE BONE!

I'M HIS COUSIN.
HIS COUSIN? ALL RIGHT! YOU WANNA PLAY WITH US?
WE'RE LEARNIN' HOW TO HANG BY OUR TAILS!
NO, THANKS. I'M ON MY WAY INTO TOWN.
HEY, MISTER! YOU KNOW TH' WAY INTO TOWN?
YEAH. WHY?
IT'S THAT WAY.
OH! RIGHT!
THANKS, KID! WHEN I COME BACK, I'LL BRING YOU A CARROT!
A CARROT? WHAT'S HE THINK WE ARE? RABBITS?
WHAT A DORK.
LUCKY THING I RAN INTO THOSE KIDS! AS SOON AS I'M BACK ON TH' RIGHT PATH, I SHOULD GET TO BARRELHAVEN IN NO TIME!

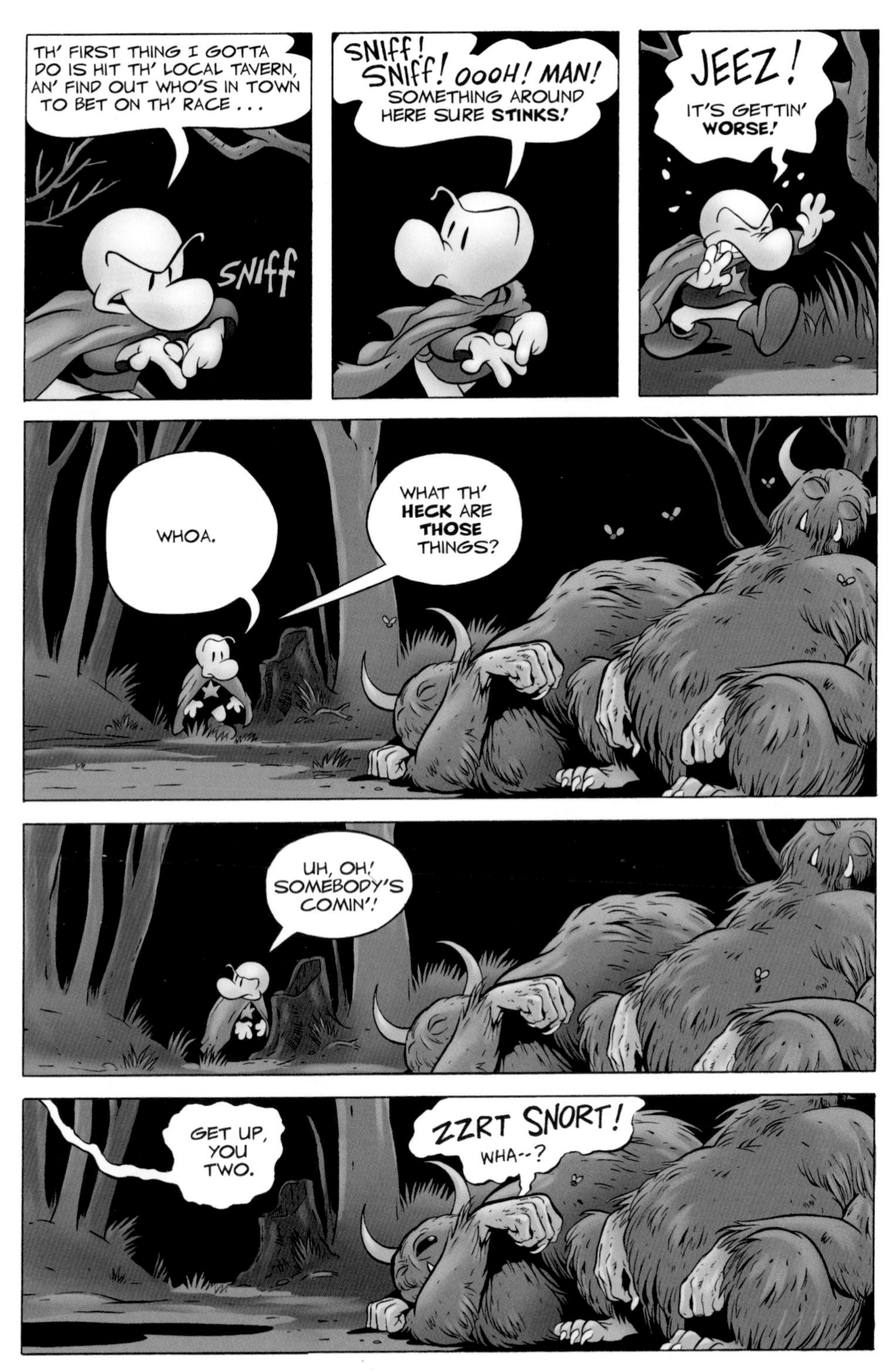
TH' FIRST THING I GOTTA DO IS HIT TH' LOCAL TAVERN, AN' FIND OUT WHO'S IN TOWN TO BET ON TH' RACE . . .
SNIFF
SNIFF! SNIFF! OOOH! MAN! SOMETHING AROUND HERE SURE STINKS!
JEEZ! IT'S GETTIN' WORSE!
WHOA.
WHAT TH' HECK ARE THOSE THINGS?
UH, OH! SOMEBODY'S COMIN'!
GET UP, YOU TWO.
ZZRT SNORT! WHA--?

GET UP BEFORE I CRUSH YOUR HEADS.
KINGDOK!
KINGDOK?
SIRE! WHAT ARE YOU DOING HERE? MAY I KISS YOUR FEET? I WISH I HAD SOME QUICHE I COULD OFFER YOU--
W-WOULD YOU LIKE SOME OF THE SMALL DEAD THING I FOUND UNDER A BUSH? I WAS SAVING HALF FOR LATER, BUT YOU'RE MORE THAN WELCOME--
QUIET! I'VE HAD SCOUTS OUT LOOKING FOR YOU TWO!
Y-YOU HAVE? HOW FLATTERING! I'M FLATTERED! ARE YOU FLATTERED?
YOU TWO ARE STARTING TO MAKE ME LOOK BAD. THE HOODED ONE HAS SUMMONED YOU BOTH TO A HIGH COUNCIL-- TONIGHT!
THE HOODED ONE--
HAS SOME-THING HAPPENED?

HE HAS RECEIVED WORD THAT THE ONE WE SEEK-- THE SMALL, BALD CREATURE WITH THE STAR ON ITS CHEST-- HAS BEEN SEEN IN THE VALLEY!
HE HAS?! BUT-- BUT--
HE WAS LAST SEEN IN YOUR TERRITORY!
COME WITH ME!
YES, SIRE! RIGHT AWAY!

EVERYTHING'S READY FOR TOMORROW. I JUST WISH I COULD SHAKE THIS **GITCHY FEELIN'** I GOT!
DID YOU FIND TH' LITTLE SQUIRT?
NO. AN' MY **BOOTS** AN' **KNAPSACK** ARE MISSING, TOO! I THINK HE WENT INTO TOWN WITHOUT US!
WE LOOKED FOR HIM, BUT THERE'S NO SIGN OF HIM ON THE ROAD. WE WENT ALL THE WAY TO OLD MAN'S CAVE BEFORE IT GOT TOO DARK. I'M SURE WE'LL FIND HIM AT THE FAIR TOMORROW.
HMM. I DON'T LIKE IT. AN' THERE'S A BAD MOON OUT TONIGHT, TOO.
RUN BACK TO TH' BARN, AN' GET YOUR BLANKET. I THINK YOU BETTER COME IN TH' HOUSE WITH US TONIGHT.
OKAY.

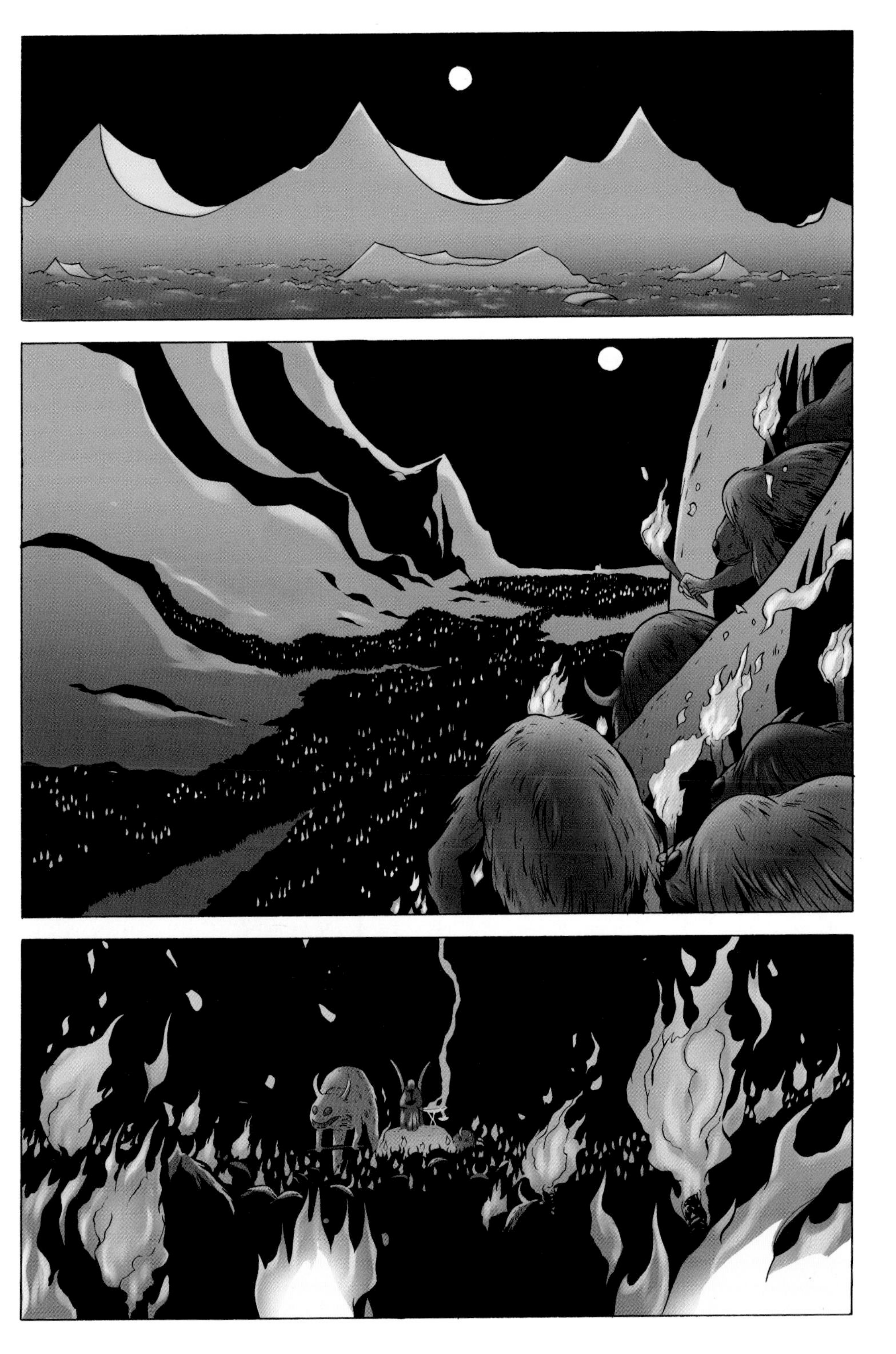

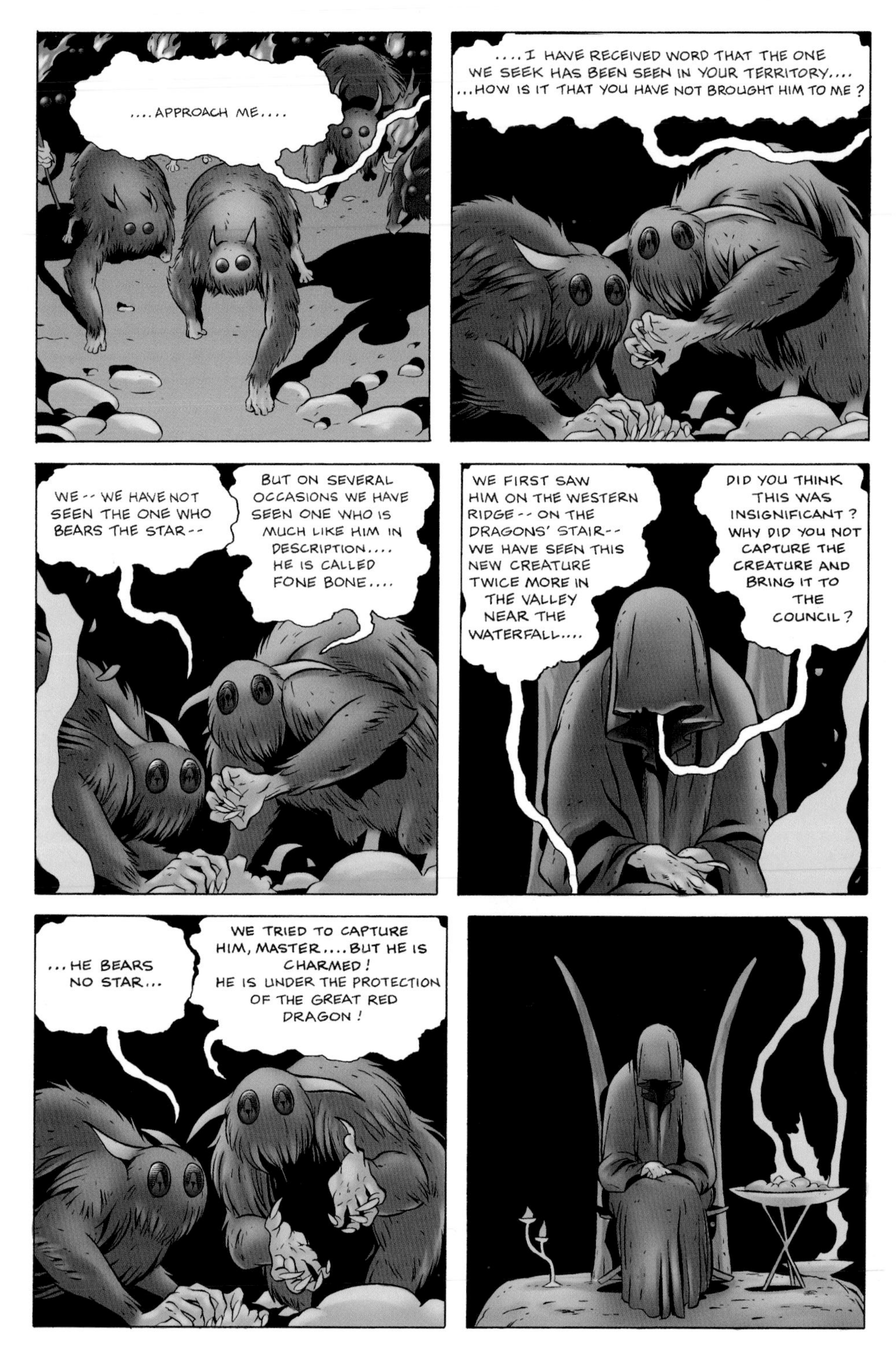
....APPROACH ME....
....I HAVE RECEIVED WORD THAT THE ONE WE SEEK HAS BEEN SEEN IN YOUR TERRITORY.... ...HOW IS IT THAT YOU HAVE NOT BROUGHT HIM TO ME?
WE -- WE HAVE NOT SEEN THE ONE WHO BEARS THE STAR --
BUT ON SEVERAL OCCASIONS WE HAVE SEEN ONE WHO IS MUCH LIKE HIM IN DESCRIPTION.... HE IS CALLED FONE BONE....
WE FIRST SAW HIM ON THE WESTERN RIDGE -- ON THE DRAGONS' STAIR -- WE HAVE SEEN THIS NEW CREATURE TWICE MORE IN THE VALLEY NEAR THE WATERFALL....
DID YOU THINK THIS WAS INSIGNIFICANT? WHY DID YOU NOT CAPTURE THE CREATURE AND BRING IT TO THE COUNCIL?
...HE BEARS NO STAR...
WE TRIED TO CAPTURE HIM, MASTER....BUT HE IS CHARMED! HE IS UNDER THE PROTECTION OF THE GREAT RED DRAGON!

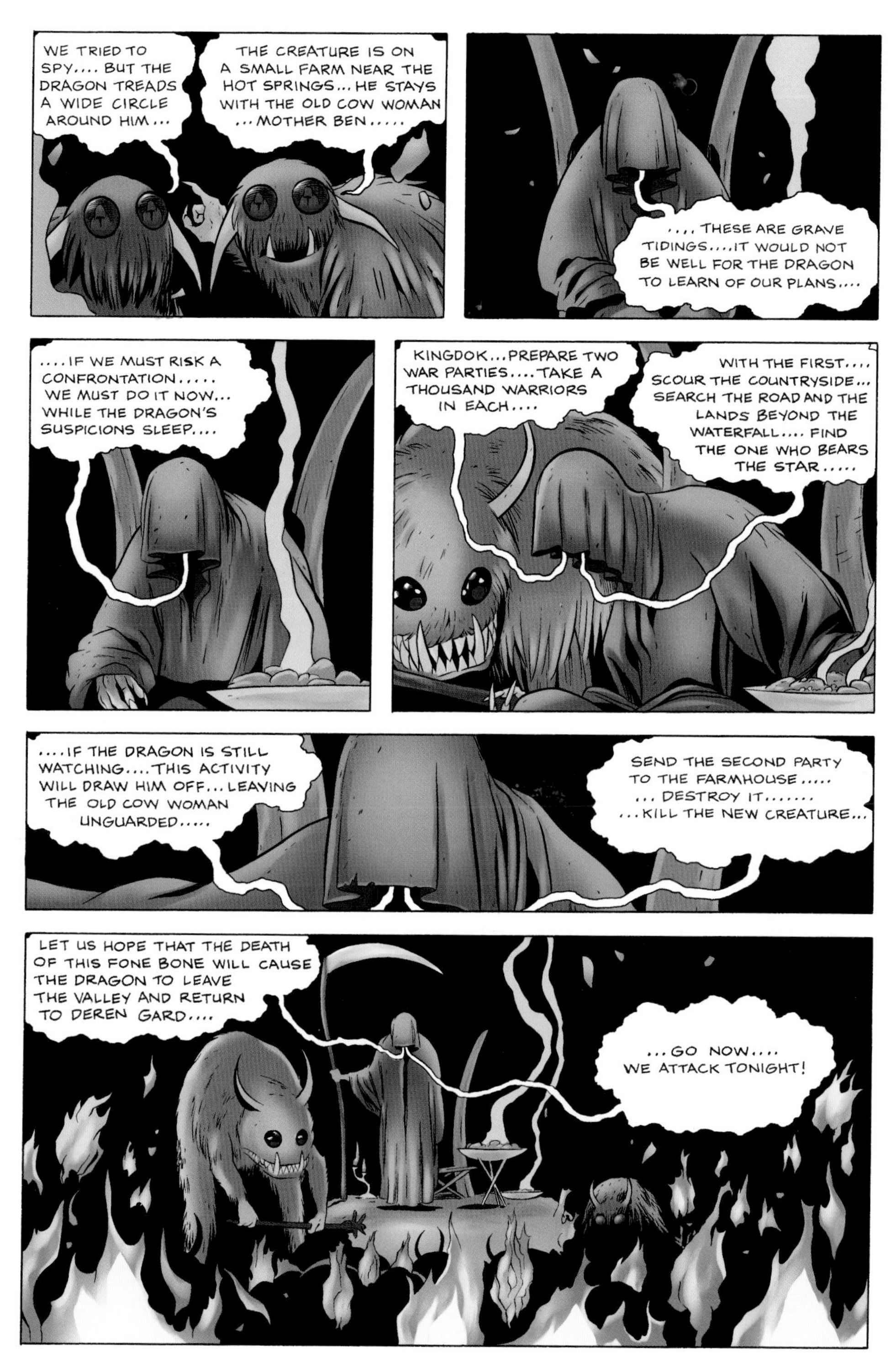
WE TRIED TO SPY.... BUT THE DRAGON TREADS A WIDE CIRCLE AROUND HIM...
THE CREATURE IS ON A SMALL FARM NEAR THE HOT SPRINGS... HE STAYS WITH THE OLD COW WOMAN ...MOTHER BEN.....
.... THESE ARE GRAVE TIDINGS....IT WOULD NOT BE WELL FOR THE DRAGON TO LEARN OF OUR PLANS....
....IF WE MUST RISK A CONFRONTATION..... WE MUST DO IT NOW... WHILE THE DRAGON'S SUSPICIONS SLEEP....
KINGDOK...PREPARE TWO WAR PARTIES....TAKE A THOUSAND WARRIORS IN EACH....
WITH THE FIRST.... SCOUR THE COUNTRYSIDE... SEARCH THE ROAD AND THE LANDS BEYOND THE WATERFALL.... FIND THE ONE WHO BEARS THE STAR.....
....IF THE DRAGON IS STILL WATCHING....THIS ACTIVITY WILL DRAW HIM OFF... LEAVING THE OLD COW WOMAN UNGUARDED.....
SEND THE SECOND PARTY TO THE FARMHOUSE..... ... DESTROY IT....... ...KILL THE NEW CREATURE...
LET US HOPE THAT THE DEATH OF THIS FONE BONE WILL CAUSE THE DRAGON TO LEAVE THE VALLEY AND RETURN TO DEREN GARD....
...GO NOW.... WE ATTACK TONIGHT!

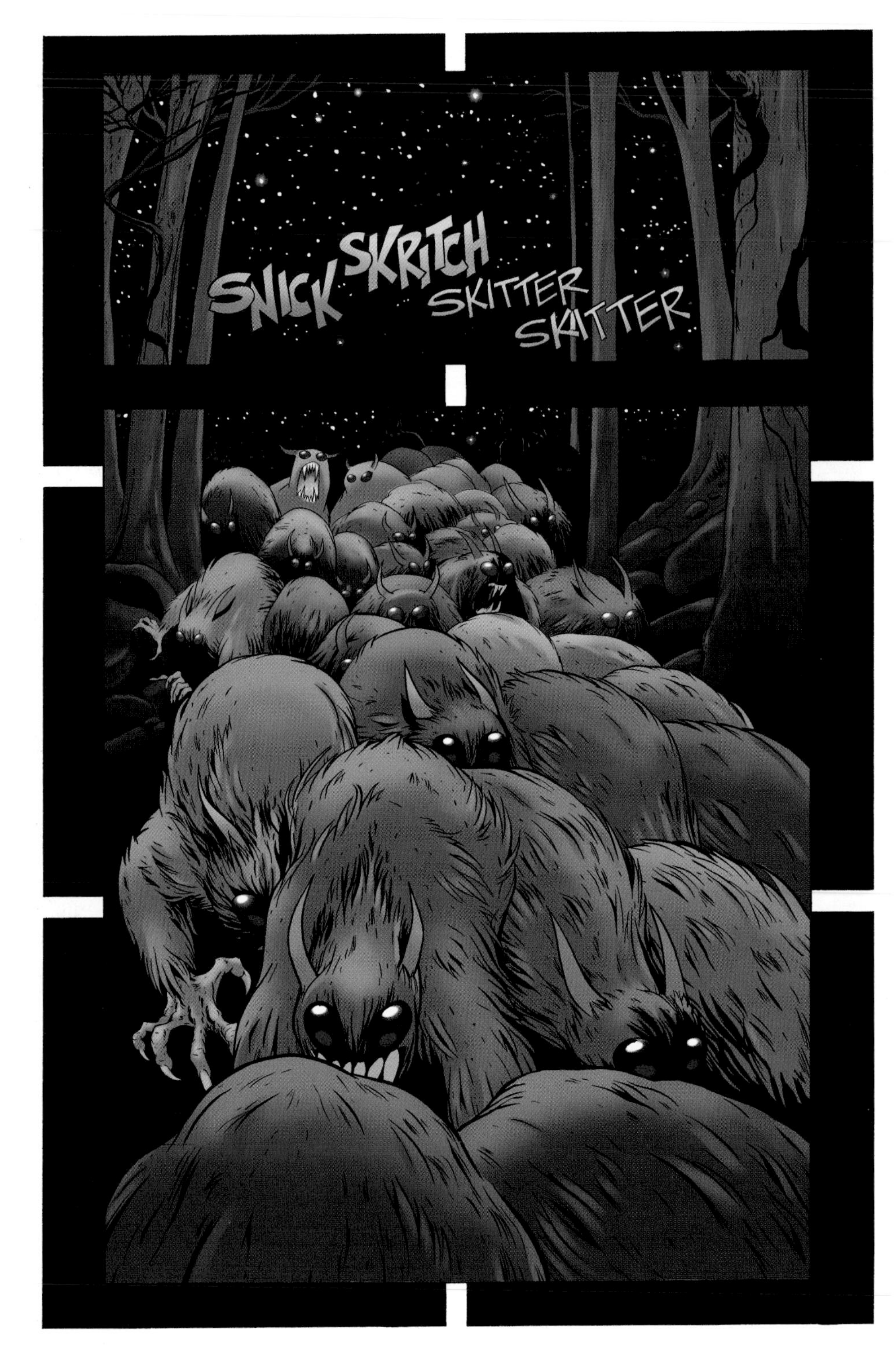
SNICK
SKRITCH
SKITTER
SKITTER

THEY'RE COMING --
RUN--
WHAT ABOUT THE COURTYARD?
THEY'VE GONE TO JOIN THEM ON THE WALLS!
FILL EVERY VESSEL WITH WATER!
THE VILLAGE IS LOST
THE GATE CANNOT HOLD MUCH LONGER
ONLY WHAT YOU CAN CARRY...
THEY'VE ENTERED THE COURTYARD
HURRY! TAKE THE CHILD!

UHHH
FONE BONE! I HAD THE DREAM AGAIN! THE RAT CREATURES WERE ATTACKING!
IT'S NO DREAM! IT'S HAPPENING!
NO --
THE RAT CREATURES HAVE SURROUNDED TH' FARM!! HURRY! GRAN'MA'S WAITING FOR US DOWNSTAIRS!

BONE
GRAN'MA?! WHAT'S GOING ON?!
WHERE ARE THEY?
THEY'VE SURROUNDED THE HOUSE . . . HURRY DOWN HERE!
DO YOU THINK IT'S SAFE TO HAVE ALL THESE LIGHTS BURNIN'? MAYBE WE SHOULD DOUSE 'EM!
NO. TH' LIGHTS ARE KEEPIN' TH' MONSTERS BACK!
IF IT WAS DARK IN HERE, AN' THE RAT CREATURES THOUGHT WE WERE ASLEEP- - WE'D BE DEAD RIGHT NOW.

HOW MANY ARE THERE?
DON'T KNOW . . . HERE, BONE. HOLD THIS!
OH, MAN!
I CAN HEAR 'EM MOVIN' AROUND OUT THERE!
THORN, DEAR . . . BRING ME A POKER FROM THE FIREPLACE - - AND YOU BETTER PUT SOME SHOES ON . . .
DO YOU HAVE A PLAN, GRAN'MA?
I HAVE AN IDEA THAT MIGHT WORK.
OKAY, CHILDREN! LISTEN CLOSELY! THIS IS WHAT WE'RE GOING TO DO . . .
- - WHEN I SAY RUN . . . . . . YOU RUN! GOT THAT?
WHAT?!
THAT'S YOUR PLAN? RUN WHERE?
READY?
HERE WE GO!

CRASSSH
SPLINTER
K-K-R-R-K-V-V-V
OKAY, KIDS! RUN!
CRUNCH
UH . . .
NOW, BONE!
WE CAN'T JUST LEAVE YOU HERE!
COME ON, FONE BONE!
DON'T WORRY ABOUT ME--
BIF!
SPLAT!
I FOUGHT TH' RATS BACK IN TH' BIG WAR!
OHMYGOSH
THUD THUD!
WAK!

OHMYGOSH

OHMYGOSH

GET UP! GET UP!

WHAT HAPPENED?
WHY ARE WE STOPPING?
Shh! WE HAVE TO GO BACK! GRAN'MA NEEDS OUR HELP!
NOW YOU'RE WORRIED ABOUT GRAN'MA?!
THERE'S TOO MANY! SHE DIDN'T KNOW THE WOODS WERE FULL OF MONSTERS!
AAAAH!

BONK!
HEY!
I'M SORRY! IT WAS A REFLEX!
AAAAARRRRRRRRR
RUN FASTER!
ME?!

the Barrel~ Haven
L. Down. Prop.
CREEEAK

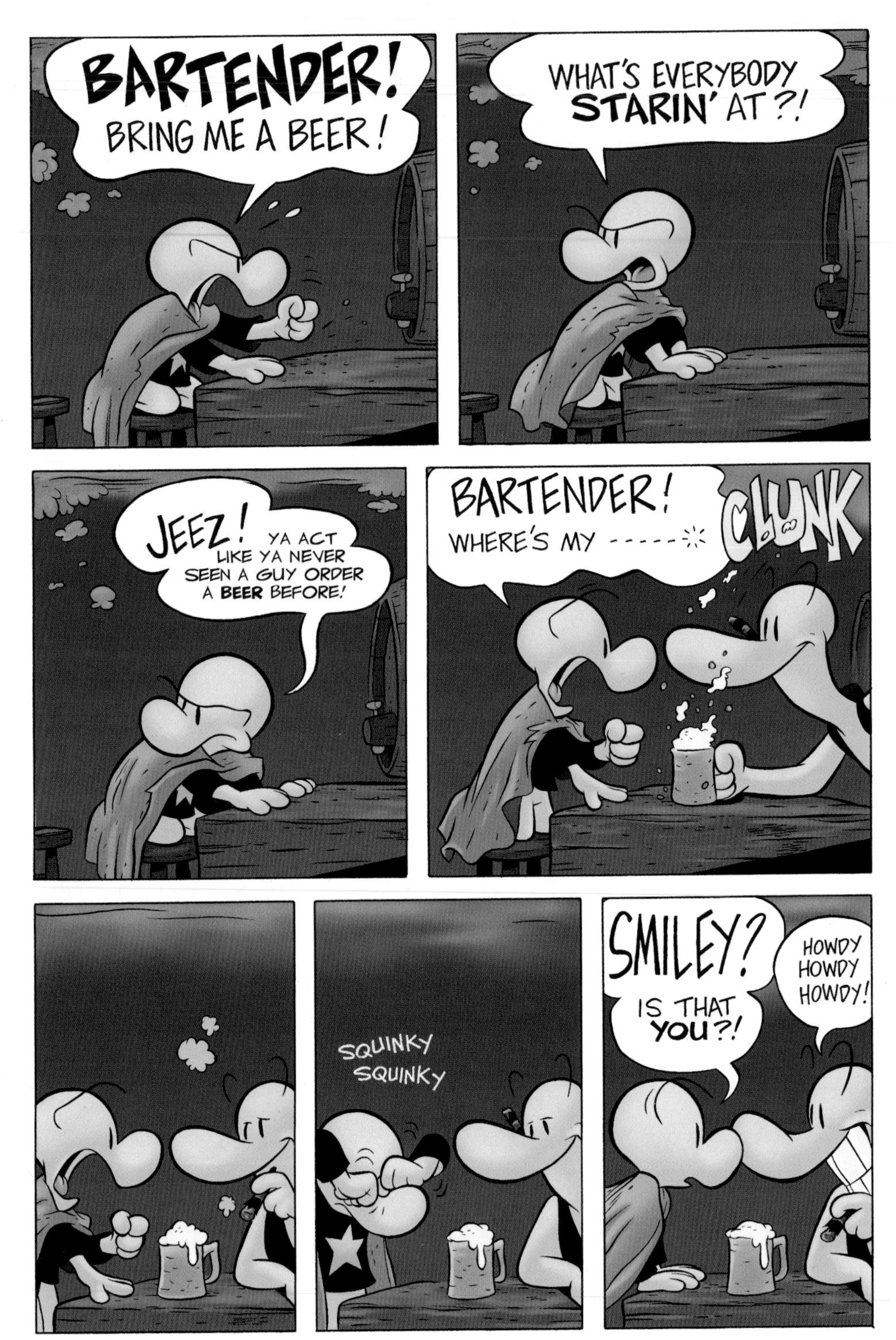
BARTENDER! BRING ME A BEER!
WHAT'S EVERYBODY STARIN' AT?!
JEEZ! YA ACT LIKE YA NEVER SEEN A GUY ORDER A BEER BEFORE!
BARTENDER! WHERE'S MY - - - - -
CLUNK
SQUINKY SQUINKY
SMILEY? IS THAT YOU?!
HOWDY HOWDY HOWDY!

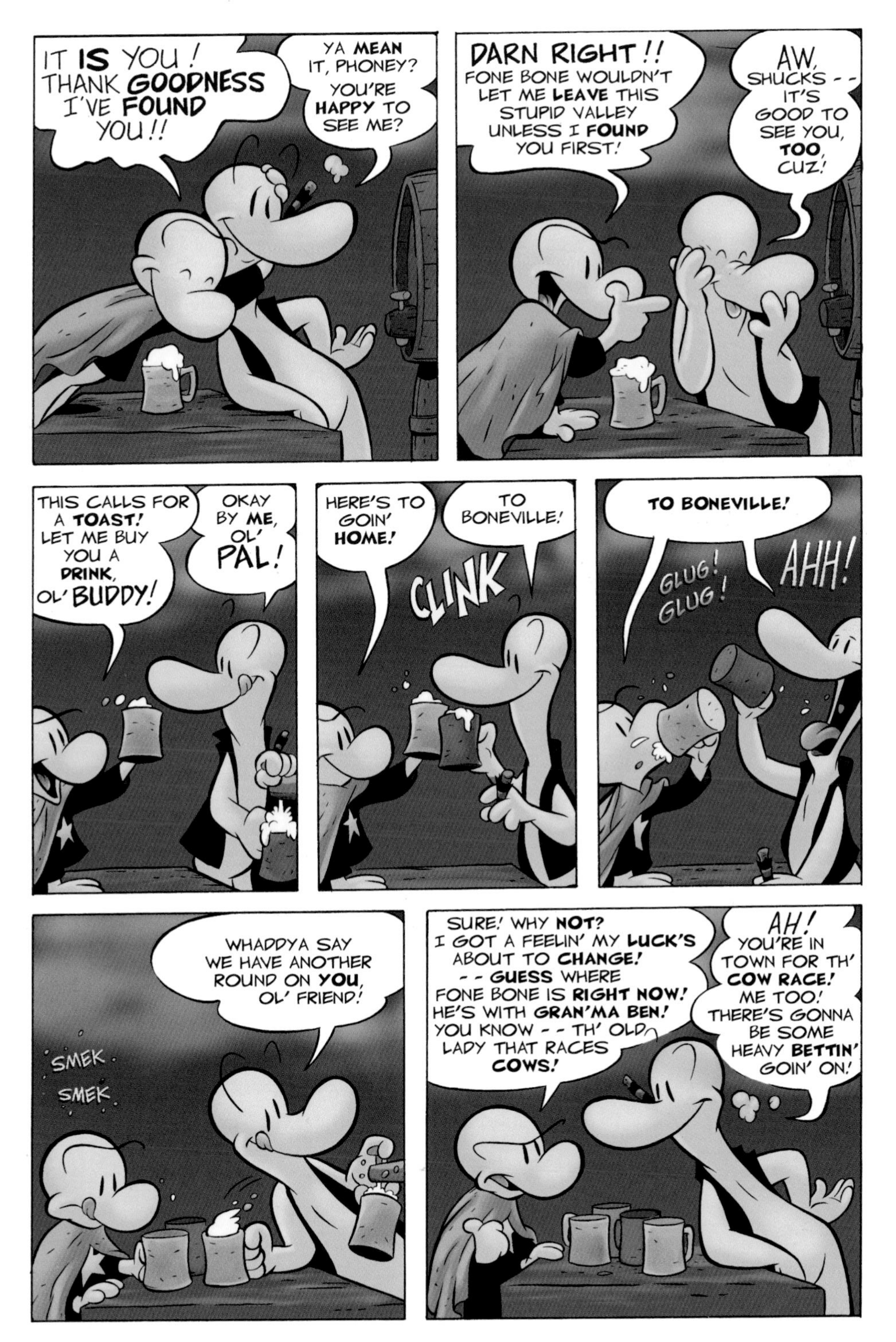

IT IS YOU! THANK GOODNESS I'VE FOUND YOU!!
YA MEAN IT, PHONEY? YOU'RE HAPPY TO SEE ME?
DARN RIGHT!! FONE BONE WOULDN'T LET ME LEAVE THIS STUPID VALLEY UNLESS I FOUND YOU FIRST!
AW, SHUCKS - - IT'S GOOD TO SEE YOU, TOO, CUZ!
THIS CALLS FOR A TOAST! LET ME BUY YOU A DRINK, OL' BUDDY!
OKAY BY ME, OL' PAL!
HERE'S TO GOIN' HOME!
TO BONEVILLE!
CLINK
TO BONEVILLE!
GLUG! GLUG!
AHH!
WHADDYA SAY WE HAVE ANOTHER ROUND ON YOU, OL' FRIEND!
SMEK
SMEK
SURE! WHY NOT? I GOT A FEELIN' MY LUCK'S ABOUT TO CHANGE! - - GUESS WHERE FONE BONE IS RIGHT NOW! HE'S WITH GRAN'MA BEN! YOU KNOW - - TH' OLD LADY THAT RACES COWS!
AH! YOU'RE IN TOWN FOR TH' COW RACE! ME TOO! THERE'S GONNA BE SOME HEAVY BETTIN' GOIN' ON!

SO I'VE HEARD!
IS ANYBODY DOIN' TH' BOOKMAKIN'?
NOT YET. . . BUT FROM WHAT I'VE PICKED UP- - YOUR FRIEND GRAN'MA IS TH' ODDS-ON FAVORITE!
GREAT! PERFECT! HOW MUCH TIME DO WE HAVE?
ONE WEEK.
EXCELLENT! I GOT AN IDEA THAT'LL MAKE US A LOTTA MONEY!
UH, OH! I HOPE THIS ISN'T GONNA BE ONE OF THOSE SILLY IDEAS YOU USED TO PULL BACK IN BONEVILLE!
WHAT?! WHAT ARE YOU TALKIN' ABOUT? WHAT SILLY IDEAS?!
REMEMBER TH' FIRST TIME YOU GOT US RUN OUT OF TOWN? YOU OPENED UP A CHAIN OF FRANCHISES - - BONE ENVIRONMENTAL: NUCLEAR REACTOR AND ENDLESS SALAD BARS!
THAT WASN'T A SILLY IDEA! TH' LETTUCE WOULDN'T SPOIL FOR DECADES!
WELL, IT WAS PRETTY SILLY!
OH, YEAH, YOU'RE A BRILLIANT JUDGE!
NOW- - WHERE ARE WE GONNA FIND A COW SUIT?
WHAT? I GET TO WEAR A COW SUIT?! COOL! HAVE ANOTHER BEER, PARTNER!

KEEP IT DOWN, YOU CORN HEAD! I DON'T WANT ANYBODY TO KNOW WE'RE TOGETHER!
oh! RIGHT! GOTCHA!
OH, NO! NOT ANOTHER ONE!! YOU BETTER BE ABLE TO PAY FOR THOSE BEERS, SHORTY!
DON'T WORRY! I'LL PRETEND I DON'T KNOW YOU... HUM TE DUM
THAT'S FIVE MUGS OF MY BEST ALE! YOU OWE ME TWO EGGS, AN' I WANT IT NOW!
RELAX, KING KONG! I'M GOOD FOR IT!
DOO, DOO!
JUST LIKE THIS OTHER IDIOT WAS GOOD FOR IT?!
OH, MY! LOOK AT ALL THESE DIRTY GLASSES!
I'VE HAD IT UP TO HERE WITH YOU DRIFTERS COMIN' INTO TOWN FOR TH' FESTIVAL -- TRYIN' TO GET BEER ON CREDIT!
QUIT BREATHIN' IN MY CUP!
IT'S MY CUP UNTIL YOU PAY ME THE TWO EGGS YOU OWE ME!!
JEEZ! WHAT A HOTHEAD! HERE! TAKE IT!

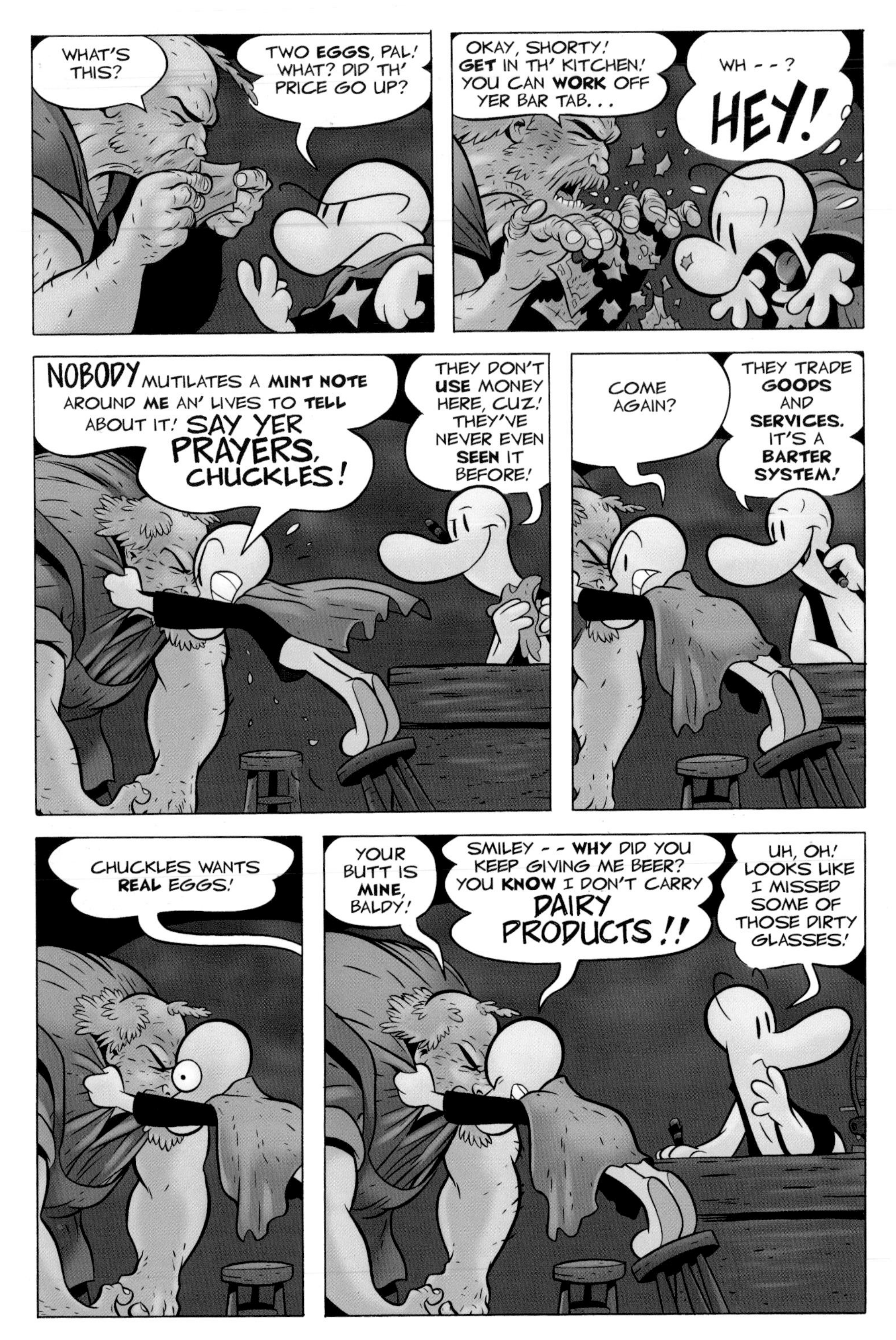
WHAT'S THIS?
TWO EGGS, PAL! WHAT? DID TH' PRICE GO UP?
OKAY, SHORTY! GET IN TH' KITCHEN! YOU CAN WORK OFF YER BAR TAB...
WH - - ?
HEY!
NOBODY MUTILATES A MINT NOTE AROUND ME AN' LIVES TO TELL ABOUT IT! SAY YER PRAYERS, CHUCKLES!
THEY DON'T USE MONEY HERE, CUZ! THEY'VE NEVER EVEN SEEN IT BEFORE!
COME AGAIN?
THEY TRADE GOODS AND SERVICES. IT'S A BARTER SYSTEM!
CHUCKLES WANTS REAL EGGS!
YOUR BUTT IS MINE, BALDY!
SMILEY - - WHY DID YOU KEEP GIVING ME BEER? YOU KNOW I DON'T CARRY DAIRY PRODUCTS!!
UH, OH! LOOKS LIKE I MISSED SOME OF THOSE DIRTY GLASSES!

CHUFF
RRRRRRR
SSSSSSSSSS

SSS
SSS

SSS
SSSSS

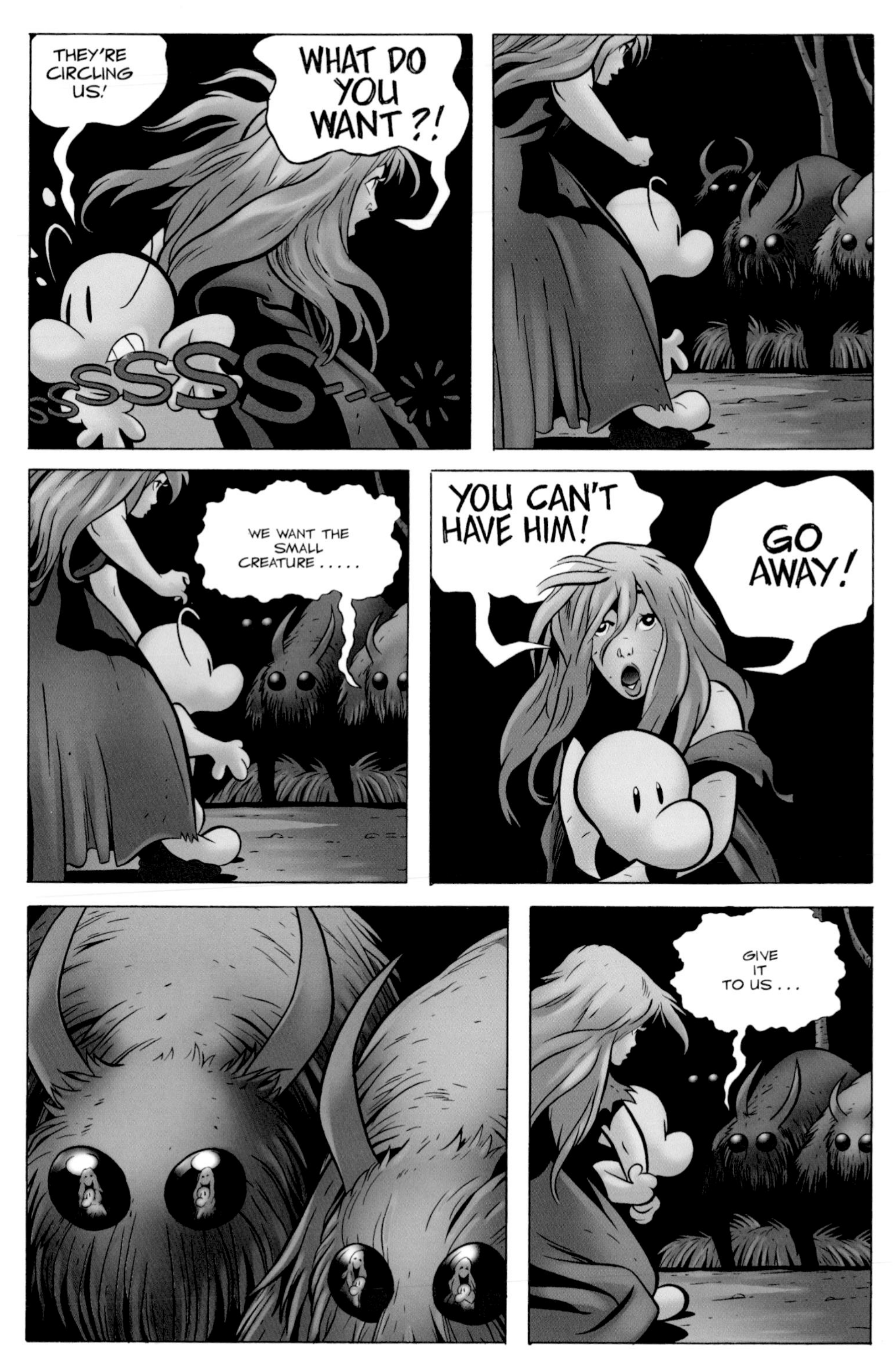
THEY'RE CIRCLING US!
WHAT DO YOU WANT ?!
SSSSSS---
WE WANT THE SMALL CREATURE . . . . .
YOU CAN'T HAVE HIM!
GO AWAY!
GIVE IT TO US . . .

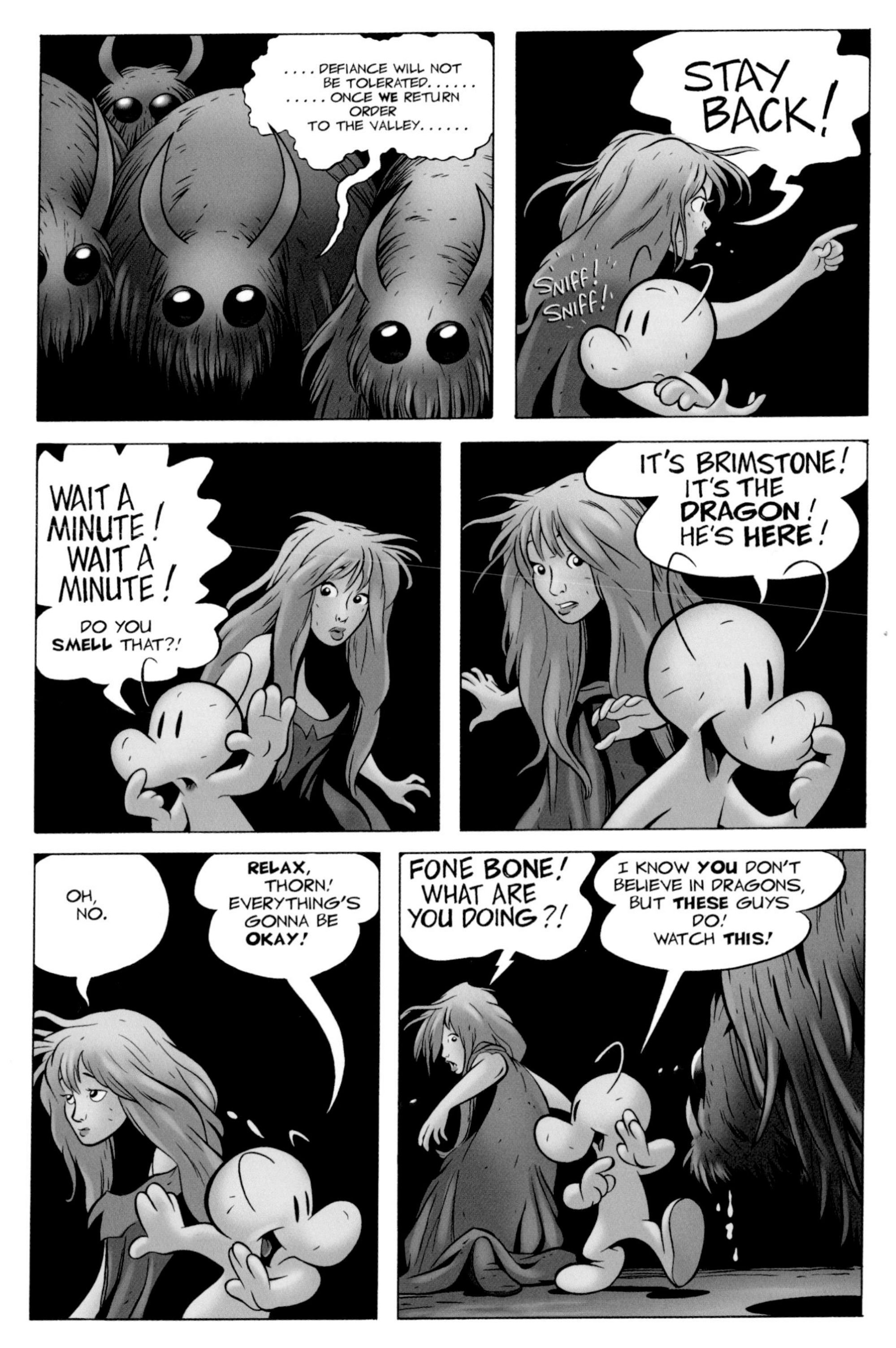
....DEFIANCE WILL NOT BE TOLERATED...... .....ONCE WE RETURN ORDER TO THE VALLEY......
STAY BACK!
SNIFF! SNIFF!
WAIT A MINUTE! WAIT A MINUTE!
DO YOU SMELL THAT?!
IT'S BRIMSTONE! IT'S THE DRAGON! HE'S HERE!
OH, NO.
RELAX, THORN! EVERYTHING'S GONNA BE OKAY!
FONE BONE! WHAT ARE YOU DOING?!
I KNOW YOU DON'T BELIEVE IN DRAGONS, BUT THESE GUYS DO! WATCH THIS!

OKAY, FELLAS! PARTY'S OVER! BREAK IT UP! LET'S GO! TH' DRAGON'LL BE HERE ANY MINUTE NOW, AN' YOU DON'T WANNA BE HERE WHEN HE SHOWS UP!
JUST THE SIGHT OF TH' DRAGON SENDS THESE GUYS INTO A PANIC! THEY RUN LIKE THEIR FUR'S ON FIRE!
ARE YOU STILL HERE? GO ON! SHOO!
I SMELL NOTHING...
WHAT ARE YOU TALKIN' ABOUT? YOU DON'T SMELL BRIMSTONE?
SSSSSS
NO.
SNIFF! SNIFF! THAT'S WEIRD! I DON'T SMELL IT ANYMORE, EITHER!
LOOK OUT!
AARR
OOF!
CHUNK

WHY, LOOK, TED. IT'S A MEETING OF THE NEW COMMUNITY LEADERS.
OOH! A TOWN MEETING! DOES WE GITS TA VOTE? I JES LOVES TA VOTE!
HISSS! STAY BACK, WORM!
OUR NUMBERS ARE TOO GREAT!
EVEN FOR YOU!
FUNNY YOU SHOULD MENTION THAT- - HOW MANY WARRIORS DO YOU HAVE BETWEEN HERE AND THE WATERFALL? A THOUSAND? TWO THOUSAND?
HIYA, BONES! HEY, THORNY! C'MON OVER HERE!

SSSSSS
I BELIEVE THIS VIOLATES OUR AGREEMENT...

YOU WOULD NOT BE SO BOLD IF KINGDOK WERE HERE!
YOU RUN AND TELL KINGDOK THAT I'M WATCHIN' HIM!

WE ARE NOT AFRAID OF YOU!!
WHO'S WE?
COMRADES! KILL THE DRA----
HISSS!

HE DID IT! YES! I TOLD YOU THERE WAS A DRAGON! I TOLD YOU!
MR. DRAGON...
MM?
...THE RAT CREATURES ATTACKED OUR FARM --
WE LEFT MY GRANDMOTHER THERE ALONE!
CLIMB ON MY BACK.
C'MON, FONE BONE!
OHMYGOSH
HOLD TIGHT!
HURRY!

STOP! STOP! LOOK!
WE'RE TOO LATE - -

BONE
I CAN'T BELIEVE IT!
THEY DESTROYED YOUR GRAN'MA'S HOUSE!
LET ME DOWN!!
WAIT A MINUTE--
...I KNOW IT LOOKS BAD, BUT WE NEED TO BE CAREFUL! WE'RE NOT GONNA HELP YOUR GRANDMOTHER BY RUSHIN' OUT IN TH' OPEN!
WE NEED TO MAKE SURE THERE'RE NO RAT CREATURES HANGIN' AROUND...

. . .THEY MIGHT BE WATCHING!
I DON'T CARE!!
GRAN'MA!
I'LL GO WITH YA, THORNY! WAIT FOR ME!
C'MON!
GRAN'MA? CAN YOU HEAR ME?
GRAN'MA BEN! WHERE ARE YOU?
CRASH
TINKLE!

THORN? IS THAT YOU, DEAR?
OH, GOOD! YOU'RE SAFE!
CRUNCH!
TINK!
GRAN'MA--!
ARE YOU ALL RIGHT?
OF COURSE I AM, DEAR! I FOUGHT TH' RATS BACK IN TH' BIG WAR! BESIDES, I WASN'T REALLY IN DANGER...
...WHEN YOU AN' BONE LEFT TH' HOUSE, ALL TH' FIGHT WENT OUT OF 'EM! I WAS MUCH MORE WORRIED ABOUT YOU!
WE ALMOST GOT CAUGHT, BUT THE DRAGON SAVED US!

A REAL DRAGON, GRAN'MA! LOOK!
I CAN SEE.
HELLO, DRAGON.
HELLO, ROSE.
IT'S BEEN A WHILE.
YEP.
WELL . . . LOOKS LIKE EVERYTHING'S UNDER CONTROL HERE. GUESS I'LL BE GOIN'.
YEP.

C'MON, TED.
GRAN'MA! WHAT ARE YOU DOING?! THE DRAGON JUST SAVED OUR LIVES!
NOT NOW, THORN. MR. BONE FROM BONEVILLE AN' I HAVE TO HAVE A LITTLE CHAT!

AND YOU HAVE A LOT OF THINGS TO DO BEFORE WE LEAVE FOR TH' SPRING FAIR!
THE FAIR?! YOU'RE NOT STILL WORRIED ABOUT YOUR COW RACE?!
WHAT ABOUT PHONEY BONE AN' SMILEY? WE HAVE TO FIND THEM!
BONE AND I WILL HITCH UP TH' CART. YOU BE A SWEETHEART AND PUT OUT TH' FIRE ON TH' ROOF!
SHE'S NOT EVEN LISTENING TO US! CAN YOU BELIEVE SHE WANTS TO GO TO TH' FAIR?!
ARE YOU KIDDING? I STILL CAN'T GET OVER TH' FACT THAT SHE HAS A FIRST NAME!
DEAR . . . I'M NOT A COMPLETE NINCOMPOOP! WE'LL BE SAFER IN TOWN! AND, WITH ANY LUCK, WE'LL BE ABLE TO FIND HIS COUSINS!
BUT - -
PLEASE, THORN! WE HAVE TO GO! WE DON'T KNOW IF THEY'RE SAFE!
YOU'RE RIGHT! I'LL TAKE CARE OF THE ROOF!
WE PACKED EVERYTHING LAST NIGHT, SO TH' LUGGAGE IS ALREADY OUT IN TH' BARN. COME JOIN US WHEN YOU GET DONE.
C'MON, BONE!
GRAN'MA? WHAT WAS THAT WITH YOU AN' TH' DRAGON? DO YOU GUYS KNOW EACH OTHER?
I'LL ASK TH' QUESTIONS! I WANNA KNOW WHY THOSE MONSTERS WERE AFTER YOU . . . AN' I WANT TH' TRUTH!
I HAVE NO IDEA! HONEST! I'VE NEVER DONE ANYTHING TO THEM!
WHAT ABOUT THAT SHIFTY COUSIN OF YOURS? YOU THINK PHONEY BONE MIGHT'VE HAD SOME DEALIN'S WITH 'EM?
NO, MA'M! WE DON'T HAVE RAT CREATURES BACK WHERE WE COME FROM!

IN FACT, WE NEVER EVEN HEARD OF RAT CREATURES BEFORE WE GOT RUN OUT OF BONEVILLE!
WELL, ACTUALLY, I WASN'T RUN OUTTA BONEVILLE - - PHONEY WAS! SMILEY AN' I JUST HELPED HIM GET AWAY!
WHAT'D HE DO?
PHONEY DECIDED HE WAS GONNA RUN FOR MAYOR! HIS CAMPAIGN SLOGAN WAS: "AN' I'VE GOT TH' MONEY TO DO IT, TOO!"
SO TH' BONES RAN HIM OUTTA TOWN FOR THAT, HUH? WELL, GOOD FOR THEM!
NO. ANYBODY CAN RUN FOR MAYOR. EVEN PHONEY!
THAT GREEDY, LITTLE LOUDMOUTH? NOT IN MY TOWN HE COULDN'T!
WELL, HE CAN IN BONEVILLE. ANYWAY, HE WANTED TO MAKE THE OFFICIAL ANNOUNCEMENT A BIG SOCIAL EVENT, SO HE DECIDED TO THROW A PICNIC DOWN ON TH' BANKS OF TH' ROLLING BONE RIVER . . .
THERE'S A BEAUTIFUL PARK THERE WITH GREEN, SLOPING LAWNS THAT STRETCH TO THE EDGE OF TH' WATER. IT'S JUST FAR ENOUGH AWAY FROM TH' HUSTLE AN' BUSTLE OF DOWNTOWN BONEVILLE THAT THERE WOULDN'T BE ANY DISTRACTIONS!

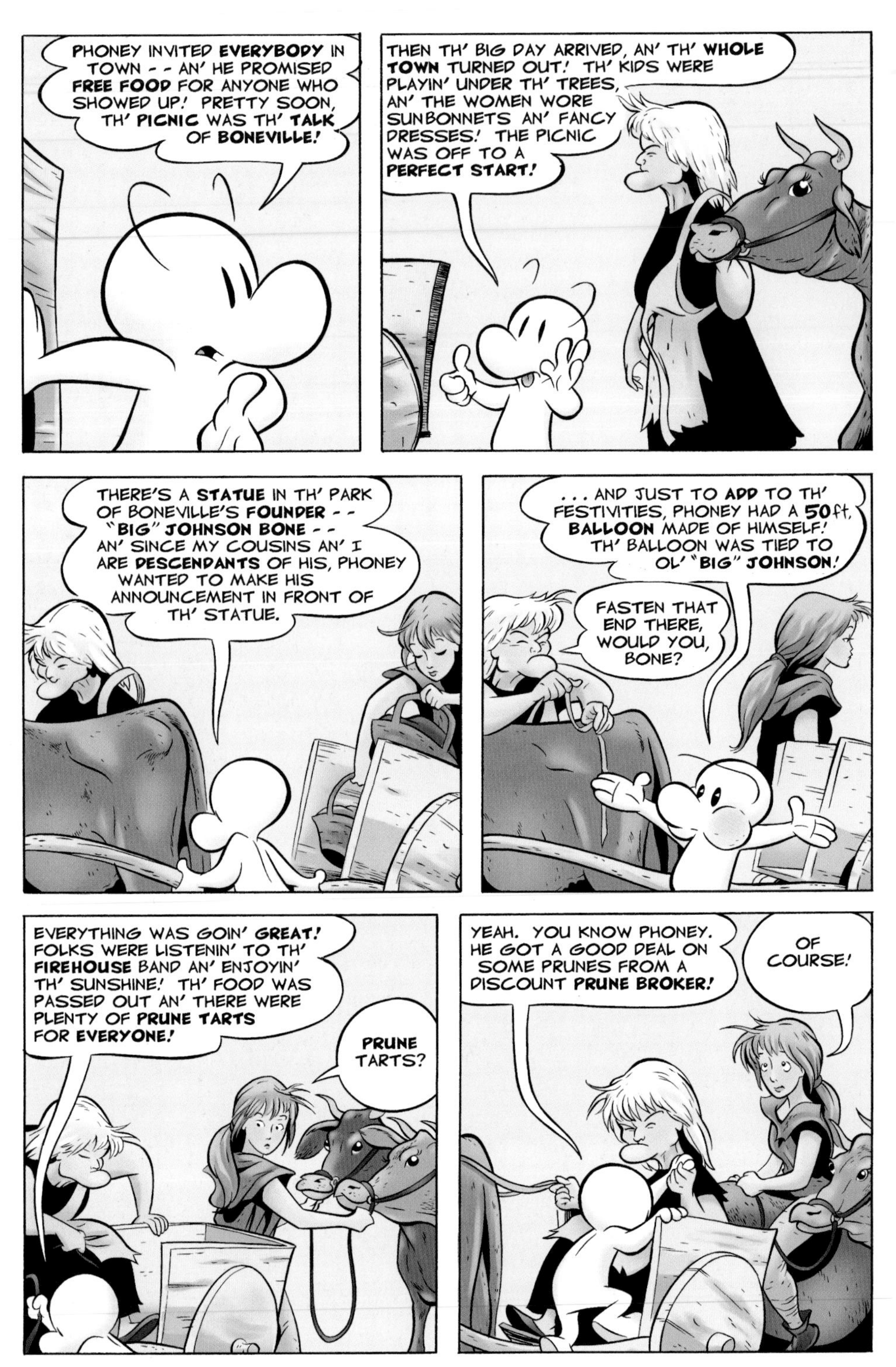
PHONEY INVITED EVERYBODY IN TOWN - - AN' HE PROMISED FREE FOOD FOR ANYONE WHO SHOWED UP! PRETTY SOON, TH' PICNIC WAS TH' TALK OF BONEVILLE!
THEN TH' BIG DAY ARRIVED, AN' TH' WHOLE TOWN TURNED OUT! TH' KIDS WERE PLAYIN' UNDER TH' TREES, AN' THE WOMEN WORE SUNBONNETS AN' FANCY DRESSES! THE PICNIC WAS OFF TO A PERFECT START!
THERE'S A STATUE IN TH' PARK OF BONEVILLE'S FOUNDER - - "BIG" JOHNSON BONE - - AN' SINCE MY COUSINS AN' I ARE DESCENDANTS OF HIS, PHONEY WANTED TO MAKE HIS ANNOUNCEMENT IN FRONT OF TH' STATUE.
. . . AND JUST TO ADD TO TH' FESTIVITIES, PHONEY HAD A 50ft. BALLOON MADE OF HIMSELF! TH' BALLOON WAS TIED TO OL' "BIG" JOHNSON!
FASTEN THAT END THERE, WOULD YOU, BONE?
EVERYTHING WAS GOIN' GREAT! FOLKS WERE LISTENIN' TO TH' FIREHOUSE BAND AN' ENJOYIN' TH' SUNSHINE! TH' FOOD WAS PASSED OUT AN' THERE WERE PLENTY OF PRUNE TARTS FOR EVERYONE!
PRUNE TARTS?
YEAH. YOU KNOW PHONEY. HE GOT A GOOD DEAL ON SOME PRUNES FROM A DISCOUNT PRUNE BROKER!
OF COURSE!

SO ANYWAY, HE MAKES THE ANNOUNCEMENT, RIGHT? HE GETS UP AND DECLARES HIS CANDIDACY FOR MAYOR OF BONEVILLE!
I STILL THINK THAT'S WHEN THEY SHOULD'VE RUN HIM OUT!
THAT'S WHEN A GUST OF WIND CAME OFF TH' RIVER AND PULLED TH' BALLOON LOOSE! THE STATUE CAME OFF ITS BASE AN' WAS DANGLIN' OFF TH' BALLOON'S ANKLE! ALL OF A SUDDEN, THIS GIANT, INFLATABLE PHONEY BONE STARTED MOVING TOWARD THE CROWD!
OH, MY!
YEAH, IT WAS AMAZING! MY FIRST-GRADE TEACHER, MISS CRAB-BONE, WAS THE FIRST TO PANIC! SHE STARTED SCREAMING AND RUNNING BACK AN' FORTH! THE BALLOON CHASED HER INTO TH' RIVER BEFORE SMILEY AND I COULD LET THE AIR OUT OF IT!
. . . IT WAS AWFUL! EVERYONE WAS STUNNED! AT FIRST NOBODY MOVED! THEY JUST SAT THERE WITH THIS LOOK OF HORROR ON THEIR FACES!
AN' THAT'S WHEN THEY RAN YOU OUTTA TOWN.
NO.
THAT'S WHEN TH' BAD PRUNES KICKED IN...

The Barrel Haven

HEY, SMILEY! TAKE THAT TUB OF GLASSES BACK TO YOUR BUDDY! WE'RE OUT OF MUGS AGAIN!
YES, SIR, MISTER DOWN!

HEY, THERE, PHONEY! LUCIUS SAYS YA GOTTA WASH THESE, PRONTO! WE GOT A LOT OF THIRSTY CUSTOMERS OUT FRONT!

OF COURSE, I MAKE SURE EVERYBODY GETS A NEW, CLEAN MUG WITH EACH DRINK!
YEAH. I NOTICED.
CLUNK

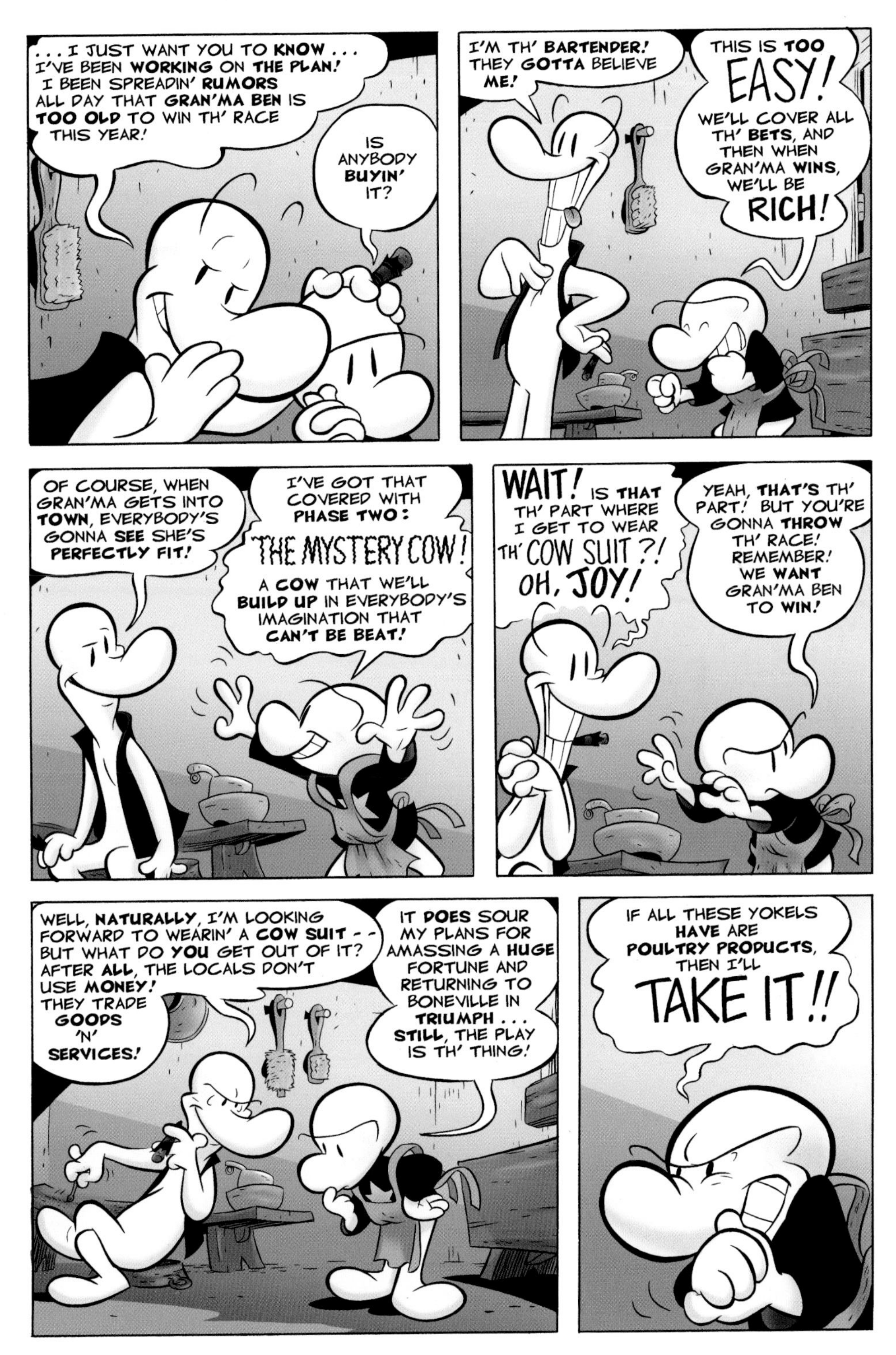
. . . I JUST WANT YOU TO KNOW . . . I'VE BEEN WORKING ON THE PLAN! I BEEN SPREADIN' RUMORS ALL DAY THAT GRAN'MA BEN IS TOO OLD TO WIN TH' RACE THIS YEAR!
IS ANYBODY BUYIN' IT?
I'M TH' BARTENDER! THEY GOTTA BELIEVE ME!
THIS IS TOO EASY! WE'LL COVER ALL TH' BETS, AND THEN WHEN GRAN'MA WINS, WE'LL BE RICH!
OF COURSE, WHEN GRAN'MA GETS INTO TOWN, EVERYBODY'S GONNA SEE SHE'S PERFECTLY FIT!
I'VE GOT THAT COVERED WITH PHASE TWO: THE MYSTERY COW! A COW THAT WE'LL BUILD UP IN EVERYBODY'S IMAGINATION THAT CAN'T BE BEAT!
WAIT! IS THAT TH' PART WHERE I GET TO WEAR TH' COW SUIT?! OH, JOY!
YEAH, THAT'S TH' PART! BUT YOU'RE GONNA THROW TH' RACE! REMEMBER! WE WANT GRAN'MA BEN TO WIN!
WELL, NATURALLY, I'M LOOKING FORWARD TO WEARIN' A COW SUIT -- BUT WHAT DO YOU GET OUT OF IT? AFTER ALL, THE LOCALS DON'T USE MONEY! THEY TRADE GOODS 'N' SERVICES!
IT DOES SOUR MY PLANS FOR AMASSING A HUGE FORTUNE AND RETURNING TO BONEVILLE IN TRIUMPH . . . STILL, THE PLAY IS TH' THING!
IF ALL THESE YOKELS HAVE ARE POULTRY PRODUCTS, THEN I'LL TAKE IT!!

BESIDES, I HAVE A HANKERIN' TO TAKE TH' PROPRIETOR OF THIS FINE ESTABLISHMENT TO TH' CLEANERS! YOU WITH ME?
SURE! IT DOESN'T MAKE ANY DIFFERENCE TO ME! BUT THEN . . . NOT MUCH DOES!
GOOD. NOW GET BACK OUT THERE AND KEEP SPREADIN' RUMORS!
AN' QUIT BRINGIN' ME DIRTY DISHES TO WASH!
PHONCIBLE P. BONE..... AT LAST I HAVE FOUND YOU.....
WHO, ME? HOW DO YOU KNOW MY NAME?
...YOU SHOULD BE GRATEFUL INDEED THAT YOUR FRIENDS INTERFERED ON YOUR BEHALF LAST NIGHT.... I AM FORCED TO USE MUCH MORE SUBTLE METHODS OF CONTACTING YOU....
WHAT TH' HECK ARE YOU TALKIN' ABOUT?
.... YOUR COUSIN FONE BONE HAS AWAKENED THE GREAT RED DRAGON.....
.... FOR THIS ...
... I WILL KILL HIM .....

WHOA! WAIT A MINUTE, PAL! YOU LEAVE FONE BONE ALONE!
...WHAT DO YOU CARE FOR FRIENDS.......? ...ALL THAT MATTERS TO YOU IS PERSONAL GAIN......
......I HAVE EVEN JEOPARDIZED MY OWN PLANS... BUT.... ....WE HAVE UNFINISHED BUSINESS, YOU AND I.....

I'M WARNIN' YOU! DON'T COME ANY CLOSER!
....I HAVE WASTED ENOUGH TIME ON YOU AS IT IS........

YEAH? LIKE WHAT?

...YOUR SOUL...

CRASH!

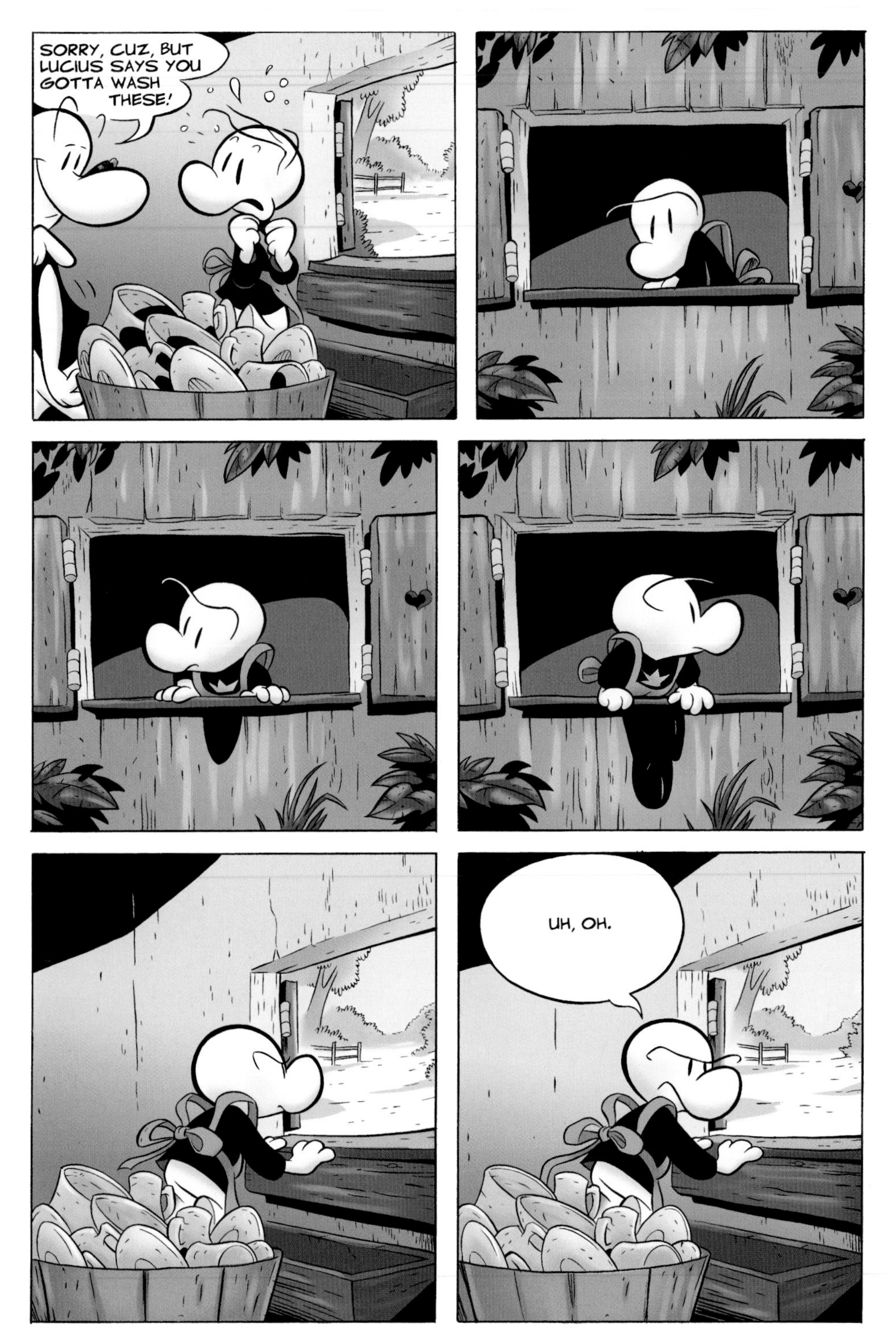
SORRY, CUZ, BUT LUCIUS SAYS YOU GOTTA WASH THESE!
UH, OH.

. . . SO THERE HE IS, OKAY? ISHMAEL'S LAYIN' IN HIS BUNK WAITIN' FOR HIS MYSTERIOUS NEW ROOMMATE TO SHOW UP . . . SUDDENLY - - AT LIKE, 3 O' CLOCK IN TH' MORNING - - TH' DOOR SWINGS OPEN . . . AN' THERE, STANDIN' IN TH' DOORWAY, WITH TH' LIGHT FROM TH' HALL BEHIND HIM, IS QUEEQUEG! AN' HE'S CARRYIN' SHRUNKEN HEADS!!
WHAT'S GOING ON, BACK THERE?
OH . . . H'LO, THORN.
ARE YOU TALKING ABOUT MOBY DICK AGAIN?
IT JUST SO HAPPENS THAT GRAN'MA LIKES TO HEAR ABOUT GOOD BOOKS! SHE APPRECIATES FINE LITERATURE!
HEY, GRAN'MA! WAKE UP!
ZZ-SNORT!
WHA - - ARE WE THERE ALREADY?
DOO-OOP!
NOT QUITE. BUT I THOUGHT I SHOULD WAKE YOU UP.

IS SOMETHING WRONG?
IT LOOKS LIKE THE ROAD IS BLOCKED UP AHEAD. THERE ARE SOME TREES DOWN ACROSS THE PATH.
STOP TH' COWS.
HMM.
THERE'S A MAN STANDING UNDER THE TREES JUST OFF TO THE SIDE OF THE ROAD. YOU SEE THAT?
WELL, I'LL BE! THAT LOOKS LIKE LITTLE JONATHAN OAKS! LET'S FIND OUT WHAT HE'S UP TO! *KIK* *KIK* LET'S GO, COW!
GOOD AFTERNOON, JON OAKS! WHAT IN TH' WORLD ARE YOU DOIN'? WHY ARE THESE TREES BLOCKIN' TH' ROAD?
GOOD DAY, GRAN'MA BEN! LUCIUS HAD US BLOCK TH' ROAD! THERE WAS SOME STRANGE DOIN'S IN TH' WOODS LAST NIGHT. TH' HAIRY MEN WERE OUT!

YES. WE SAW THEM. MAY WE PASS?
OH, YES, MA'M! COME AROUND TH' END, HERE!

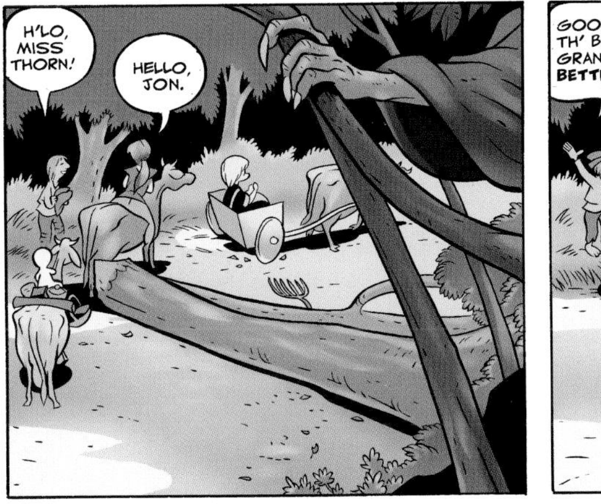
H'LO, MISS THORN!
HELLO, JON.

GOOD LUCK WITH TH' BIG RACE, GRAN'MA! EVERYONE'S BETTIN' ON YA!
THANK YOU, DEAR!

THORN?
YES, FONE BONE?

I WANT TO THANK YOU FOR STICKIN' WITH ME LAST NIGHT . . . I DON'T KNOW WHY THOSE RAT CREATURES WERE AFTER ME - - BUT THEY WOULD'VE GOT ME FOR SURE IF YOU HADN'T STOOD UP TO 'EM!

OF COURSE WE STUCK TOGETHER! WE'RE FRIENDS, AREN'T WE?
HURRY UP, NOW, KIDS! WE'RE HERE!

the Barrel~Haven
L. Down Prop.
WELL, WELL . . . IT'S ABOUT TIME!
HELLO, LUCIUS!
HOW YA DOIN', ROSIE? WAS TH' ROAD SAFE? I WAS WORRIED ABOUT YA!
TH' ROAD WAS CLEAR . . . EXCEPT FOR YOUR ROADBLOCK!
OH! I GOT SOMETHIN' FOR YA! HERE! I BEEN SAVIN' IT IN MY POCKET ALL DAY!
OH, AREN'T YOU SWEET!
...WELLL..... I HAD A LITTLE EXTRA TIME ON MY HANDS THIS MORNING . . .
. . . I GOT A COUPLE OF DEADBEATS INSIDE TAKIN' CARE OF TH' CUSTOMERS - - IN FACT, THEY LOOK A LOT LIKE THIS LITTLE FELLA YOU GOT HERE.
THEY DO?!

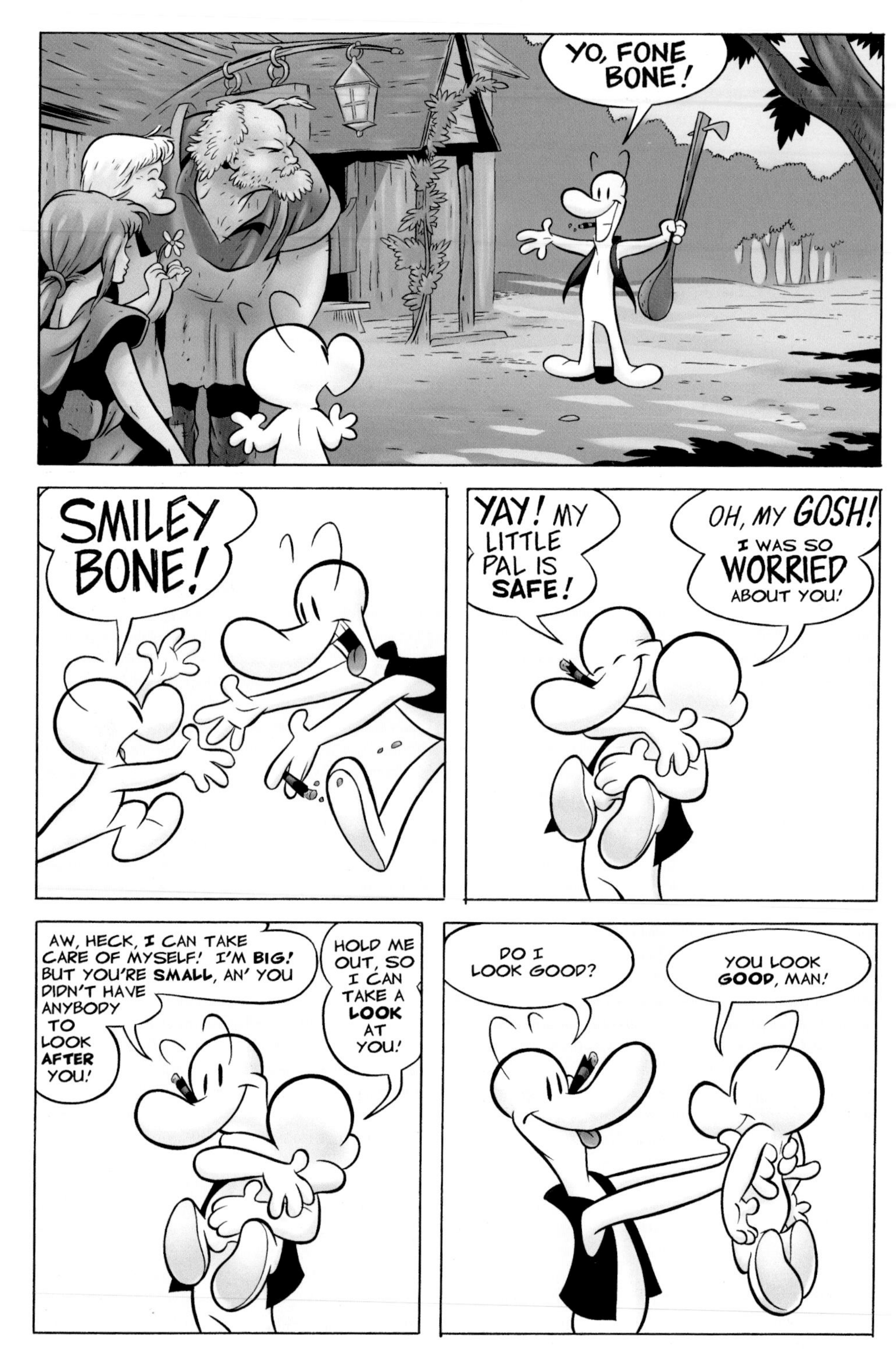
YO, FONE BONE!
SMILEY BONE!
YAY! MY LITTLE PAL IS SAFE!
OH, MY GOSH! I WAS SO WORRIED ABOUT YOU!
AW, HECK, I CAN TAKE CARE OF MYSELF! I'M BIG! BUT YOU'RE SMALL, AN' YOU DIDN'T HAVE ANYBODY TO LOOK AFTER YOU!
HOLD ME OUT, SO I CAN TAKE A LOOK AT YOU!
DO I LOOK GOOD?
YOU LOOK GOOD, MAN!

WHERE'S PHONEY?
HE'S RIGHT INSIDE! I'LL CALL HIM OUT!
NOW, JUST A MINUTE! I DON'T WANT EVERYBODY OUT HERE! WHO'LL TAKE CARE OF TH' CUSTOMERS?
LET 'EM GO, LUCIUS! THESE BOYS HAVEN'T BEEN TOGETHER FOR MONTHS!
THOSE BOYS OWE ME A LOTTA EGGS, ROSIE . . . .
OH, ALL RIGHT . . . CALL HIM OUT! BUT THEN GET BACK TO WORK!
THANKS, YA BIG LUG!
HEY, PHONEY! C'MON OUT! FONE BONE'S HERE!

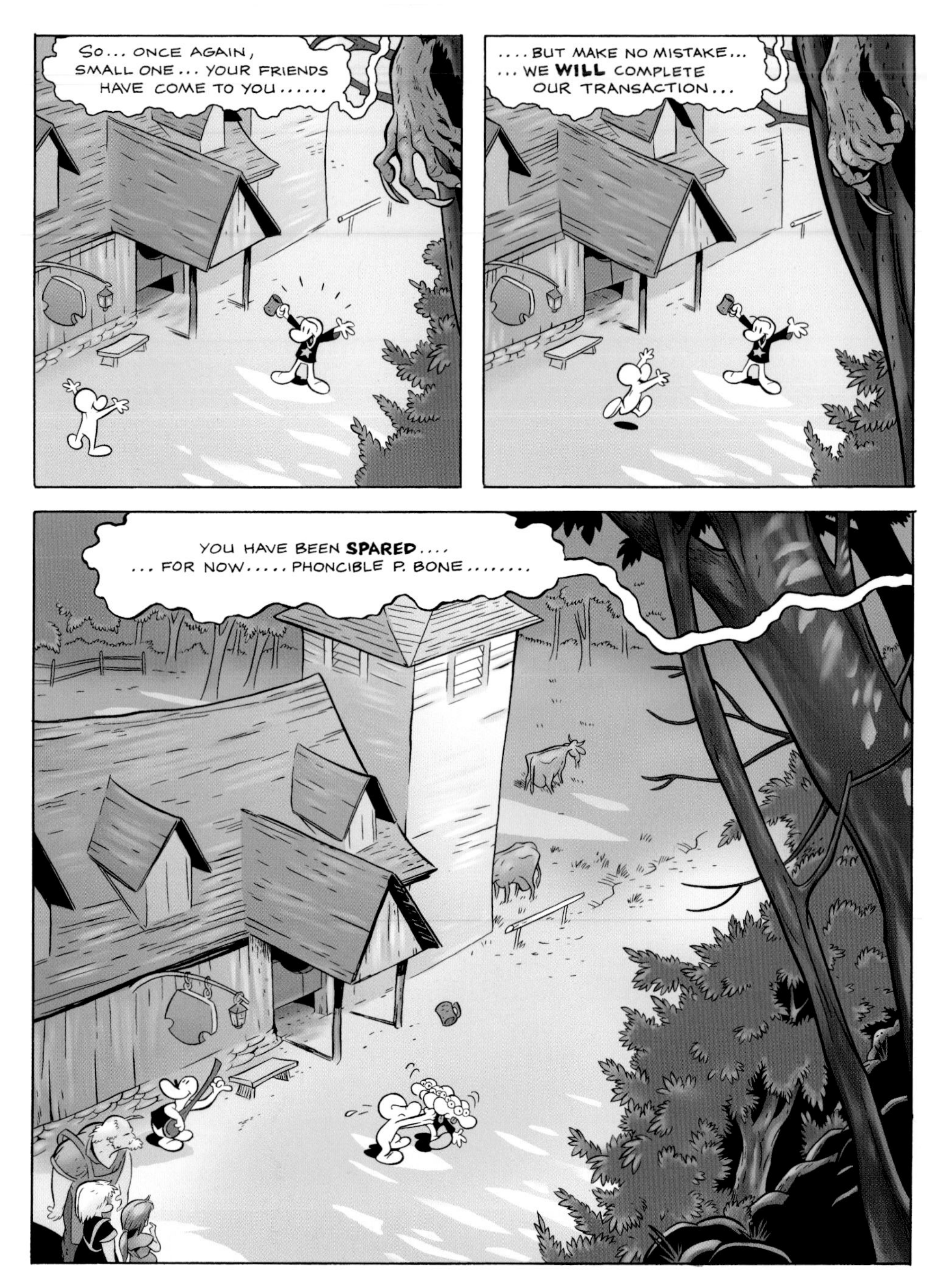
So... ONCE AGAIN, SMALL ONE... YOUR FRIENDS HAVE COME TO YOU......
....BUT MAKE NO MISTAKE... ...WE WILL COMPLETE OUR TRANSACTION...
YOU HAVE BEEN SPARED.... ...FOR NOW..... PHONCIBLE P. BONE........

About JEFF SMITH

JEFF SMITH was born and raised in the American Midwest. He learned about cartooning from comic strips, comic books, and watching animated shorts on TV. After four years of drawing comic strips for Ohio State University's student newspaper and cofounding Character Builders animation studio in 1986, Smith launched the comic book *BONE* in 1991. Between *BONE* and other comics projects, Smith spends much of his time on the international guest circuit promoting comics and the art of graphic novels.

More about BONE

Instant classics when they first appeared in the U.S. as underground comic books in 1991, the *BONE* books have since garnered 38 international awards and sold a million copies in 15 languages. Now, Scholastic's GRAPHIX imprint is publishing full-color graphic novel editions of the nine-book *BONE* series. Look for the continuing adventures of the Bone cousins in *The Great Cow Race*.